Life Begins *at* Sixty-Two *and a* Half

MARK DAYDY

Previously published as
The Unforgettable Coco Vincenza

This is a work of fiction. All names, characters, locations and incidents are products of the author's imagination, or have been used fictitiously. Any resemblance to actual persons living or dead, locales, or events is entirely coincidental. No part of this book may be reproduced without prior written permission from the author.

Copyright © 2024 MARK DAYDY

All rights reserved.

ISBN: 9798328665377

Cover design by MIKE DAYDY

BY THE AUTHOR

Life Begins at Sixty-Two and a Half

The Golden Oldies' Club

Olivia Holmes Has Inherited a Vineyard

Olivia Holmes Meets Luke and Alice

Lucy Holt Gets Involved

Those Lazy, Hazy, Crazy Days of Summer

Cathy & Chris Under Siege

Christmas Presents (A Cathy & Chris novella)

London Calling

The Girl Who Lived by the River

One

The wind whipped up on Shawcross beach, blowing Grace Chapman's salt and pepper locks around. At the same time, a breaking wave raced in and covered her sandals, dragging her feet an inch or so beneath the shingle.

Grace was clutching a black plastic urn, from which she would scatter Aunt Jen's ashes over the water, only she didn't want a sudden gust adding unwanted sprinkles to that elderly man's ice cream farther up the beach.

"Grace? Are you okay?"

Brushing her hair out of her eyes, she turned to Bev Sullivan, her best friend, standing back from the shoreline.

"I'm fine."

She turned back to the water. She would do it now. She would scatter Aunt Jen's ashes and say farewell to the last of the older generation.

It wasn't easy, of course. Under a half-blue, half-cloud late-July sky, holidaymakers were out in force enjoying the South Devon seaside. Some of them were nearer than Grace would have liked, especially three children playing with a beach ball who seemed more interested in the woman with the black plastic pot than their game.

It had to be this way though. The benches at the back of the beach had been eighty-year-old Aunt Jen's regular lunchtime spot. She had also been an occasional trousers-rolled-up paddler too. Therefore, this beach, at lunchtime, on the boats-only side of the line of buoys, was an appropriate place for dispersal. It was just that Grace had spent most of her life not drawing attention to herself.

Of course, Aunt Jen had been the opposite. A can-do, happy-go-lucky sort. Hence the scattering of her ashes on the water being the perfect way to see her off. At least it had seemed so when Grace thought of it that morning while sipping a peppermint infusion from a Harry Potter mug.

"Grace?"

"I'm fine," she called back without turning.

Good ol' Bev.

A couple of months back, Grace confessed how she sometimes wished she could have a little magic in her life. Next day, Bev bought her the mug.

She looked again to see if anyone was paying her any attention, but she was a sixty-two-year-old woman in a muted floral summer dress – the kind of beach-goer people generally ignored. Apart from the curious youngsters, any adults splashing in the waves farther along the shore were preoccupied with their own activities, as was right. After all, for most people, Shawcross was a summer getaway. For Grace though, it was home.

That said, the wind could get up at Shawcross. Certainly, spreading ashes was proving trickier than anticipated. It was clearly a matter of waiting for a lull and then tipping them out of the urn. Well, perhaps not tipping. She didn't want to dump her aunt's remains in a visible mass. That wouldn't be very spiritual. No, she would have to wait until she could shake a thin dusting over the water's surface.

Suddenly, the wind dropped.

Go, go, go…

She prepared to act.

The wind whipped up again.

Perhaps she could come back later.

Just then, a memory struck. This beach and a determination to do something important. Two very different reasons for being here separated by more than forty years.

How time flies.

She thought of her mum, who passed away when Grace was fifteen. Mum had belonged to the church choir and a poetry society and occasionally had her work published in a couple of church and poetry society newsletters. When she died, teen Grace wrote a poem for the service. A humorous one about her mum's childhood, recounting skipping ropes and friends, and summer days without end.

Grace backed out of reciting it though to spare the mourners any embarrassment.

The wind dropped again.

She felt the weight of the container in her hand. She wasn't just waving off the old guard, she was waving off their era too.

"Well, Aunt Jen… and Mum… and all of you. I wish there was some way I could give the old days a better send-off. Any suggestions for something grand and amazing would be welcome."

She waded a good way in and began to scatter. The current would soon take the ashes out to sea.

"Bye, Aunt Jen. I miss you."

It didn't take long to complete the task. That entire generation – they were all gone now. All the things they did and lived through.

Life suddenly seemed short.

Grace tucked the empty container into her shoulder bag and tramped out of the water and back up the beach. Her next stop would be Aunt Jen's flat to start the process of clearing it out. She wasn't looking forward to that. There was the sentimental side to it, but also the fact her aunt did like keeping things.

Bev's smile was somewhere between happy and sad. And under her cropped silver hair, as always, the expression in those blue eyes matched her smile, because that's what you got with genuine souls.

"Are you okay, Grace?" she asked.

"I'm fine, Bev. Thanks for everything you did for Aunt Jen these past few years. Helping her with shopping and what have you."

"She lived fifty yards down the street from me. It was no bother at all."

"I know, but thanks. That said, I'd like to do something a little out of character."

"It's a bit early for a booze-up."

"No, I mean we don't go on forever, so for once in my life I'd like to do something… well… remarkable."

"Next door's daughter does that," said Bev as they reached the benches at the back of the beach and took a seat. "Last week she went on a date wearing Barbie pink boots, an army camouflage dress, and goth makeup."

"I'm not talking about appearances. I'm talking about offering my time in a meaningful way."

"Good idea. Once you've finished at your aunt's, you can help me. I'm due to sort through the stuff in the loft, but Jez reckons we should just throw it all away."

"Bev, I mean I want to honour Aunt Jen's memory by doing something significant. You know, something that'll make a difference."

"Right… okay… I'm still not sure what you mean, but don't let me stop you."

"How do people do that?"

"What, make a difference? Let me see… Lesley Pearce does it by running marathons. She's raised thousands for that diabetes charity."

"Yes, exactly! Lesley Pearce running marathons for charity is absolutely what I'm talking about. I'd like to make a Lesley Pearce kind of difference, but without the running."

"The Aunt Jen Memorial Short Walk?"

Grace looked out to sea.

"I doubt that would raise as much as Lesley."

"No, I suppose not."

"I don't mind putting in a big effort, Bev. It just needs to be something that would raise a lot of money without putting me in hospital. There must be a way."

"Oh, there will be. I'm sure of it. It's just…"

Grace turned to her friend. "What?"

"Well, don't take this the wrong way, but you're probably talking in the heat of the moment."

"No, I'm serious."

"Honestly, it's great to hear. It's just that I've never heard it before in the fifty years I've known you."

"Yes, well, things are about to change," insisted Grace. "I want to achieve something meaningful and worthwhile. Something that will make a difference."

Bev frowned a little.

"Are you sure about this?"

"Yes, I am."

"And this *something*… you'll see it through to the bitter end?"

"Yes, absolutely."

"Only, you're normally a creature of the background, a lurker on the periphery, a non-speaking shepherd in the school Nativity play…"

"Yes, I know… but for one time only, I'm going to celebrate Aunt Jen's life by moving to the front of the stage. I've no idea what I'll do, and no idea how I'll achieve it, but this is happening. If I back out, you can denounce me to everyone in the Sunny Side Up Café as a pathetic, miserable fraud."

Bev smiled broadly.

"Well, this is an unexpected turn of events. An all-new Grace Chapman is going to make a difference. I can hardly wait."

Two

The following morning, in bright sunshine, Grace brought her midnight blue Polo to a halt outside Crowthorne Court, a late-Victorian red brick block of flats typical of the north side of town by the seafront. She had come to remove all evidence of her aunt having lived there for half a century, which wouldn't be easy.

Locking the car, Grace headed for the communal entrance – a familiar scene that now felt wildly different, as if her permanent invitation to enter had been withdrawn.

She hesitated for a moment, and saw herself all those years ago helping Aunt Jen move in.

"Come on," Jen was saying. "My home is your home."

As a twelve-year-old, Grace had shared her aunt's enthusiasm for the move. Of course, over the years, she came to realise it had been a brave face rather than excitement. Aunt Jen had unexpectedly lost her husband,

Uncle Rex to illness and moving in represented a fresh start. Fifty years on, the fresh start had reached its conclusion.

Grace opened the communal front door and entered the stone-floor lobby. A faint whiff of bleach lingered as she walked past the stone stairway and along a short corridor to number 4, her aunt's ground floor flat.

She turned the key and pushed the door. And there was that familiar aroma of old books, potted plants and beeswax.

Most of Aunt Jen's stuff was vintage – she'd had a liking for dark wood furniture, mainly Victorian or Edwardian, and had never been to Ikea. With plenty of finishing touches, from plump cushions to elegant lamps, the flat always felt welcoming and warm.

Grace had lived there herself for six years following her mum's passing. There hadn't been an option to live with her dad – he'd fled the scene years before and had begun again with a new wife. Funny how Grace herself was now experiencing something similar, with her own husband currently living with a woman called Tiff.

"Tea, I think," she uttered. That had always been the first rule in Aunt Jen's home. Being sensible, Grace had brought some milk, as the place had been unoccupied for a while.

A few minutes later, perched on Aunt Jen's Chesterfield sofa, Grace sipped her hot drink and listened intently to the silence. Perhaps her aunt had only popped out to the shops and, any minute now, would come bustling through the front door armed with fresh bread and gossip.

But no, that wouldn't happen. The silence was permanent – at least until a new tenant took over.

She thought about that. People stressing and straining for years over finances, decorating and choosing furniture… and making it the place they could call home… a place where home and occupant would eventually become intertwined… until the next person took over.

No doubt, a hundred years from now, somebody would step over the threshold of number 4, Crowthorne Court for the first time and see it as a new and exciting adventure, with not a single thought for Aunt Jen who was once part of the fabric.

Grace put her cup down on the dark oak coffee table and went to the mantlepiece. Here, twenty or so framed photographs of varying sizes filled every inch of space.

In one, Aunt Jen was smiling amongst friends on a girls' night out. She looked thirty or so. Such colourful 1970s outfits. Such happy faces.

Next to this was a professional black and white photo of a singer called Lizzie La Grange, who smouldered at the camera like a 1950s Hollywood star. It almost overshadowed a smaller, coloured photo of a woman in her forties called Helen, who had worked with Aunt Jen for many years. Then came another girls' night out photo with most of the same faces as before, but twenty years older.

There were a few more before she came to a long-haired eighteen-year-old Grace staring out from a framed Polaroid. The day that photo was taken, she learned she was adopted. Aunt Jen was Mum's younger sister. It was she who handed over the birth certificate that named her real mother, Mary Smith, aged seventeen. What followed was a lifetime of unanswered questions because Aunt Jen knew nothing about Mary Smith. Over the years, Grace had often pondered the pros and cons of looking into it. The thing was though, there had always been a perfect balance between wanting to know and not wanting to know.

"Right," she told herself, "this is *not* a self-clearing flat."

But where to start? That was the problem.

Food…?

The freezer contained one single-portion microwavable fish pie. Should she take it home? It felt odd. Would she be able to eat her aunt's meal without feeling spooked? Besides, wasn't her own small freezer already full of dinners-for-one? She thought of the local food bank, but that lacked a freezer.

She had a rethink. Were there any non-edible things she could take in the car? There were, of course – probably enough to fill ten cars.

"Come on," she urged herself. "Time to make room for someone else's life."

She decided on clothes. Being a most personal aspect of her aunt's life, she had wanted to put it off, but it actually made sense to get this out of the way early.

In the bedroom, she was immediately drawn away from the wardrobe by a photo album resting on the bedside table. Perhaps her aunt had sat in bed and gone through it in her final hours before being taken to the hospital.

Grace sat on the edge of the bed and opened a treasure trove of birthdays, summer get-togethers, Christmas festivities and so on. One with Aunt Jen and herself on a beach caught her eye. Young Grace was smiling proudly about something. There was no way to tell what, but the smile was one of joy. How happy she must have been in that long-forgotten moment. She removed the photo from the plastic wallet and flipped it over. Aunt Jen had written, 'Goodrington Sands, Autumn 1970.'

She considered it. An autumnal Goodrington – just a few miles around the bay. She would have been eight years old in a world now lost to memory.

She slid the photo back into place. A physical album was old fashioned these days. Now photos were kept on a phone or a computer. But she liked the look and feel of photos you could hold.

"Wardrobe!" she instructed herself.

She put the photo album down and began assessing the clothes that were hanging up. Anything that looked good would be bagged up for a charity shop. Anything that looked tired or shabby, she would pile on the bed to be thrown away. She was about to get started but changed her mind.

In the front room, she opted for a cabinet full of books. The first to stand out was one Grace had bought for her aunt as a sixtieth birthday present twenty years ago: 'How to be Active in Later Life.'

That might come in handy.

She put it by her bag. It would bolster her own small library of self-help books. All unread.

Grace had always admired her aunt. She'd had an ability to get on with things. And she had always helped others. When she retired from work, she joined a local am-dram group. Within weeks, she had taken over their publicity and admin. She was a very focused person. She got things done.

Within a few minutes, Grace had most of the books stacked on the coffee table – and wished she'd left them in the cabinet.

Next, she went through the two drawers in the sideboard, which seemed to hold six drawers' worth of stuff. In truth, it was driving her mad. There seemed to be no way to make any progress. Should she ask Bev for help?

She went to the window, where a blue sky reminded her that the outside world was enjoying sunshine, fresh air and freedom, while she was stuck inside going through dusty old papers. But no, she was capable of dealing with this herself.

She turned to face the room once more. It was time to close down Aunt Jen's life. But it made her wonder. What of her own life? Would there be a final meaningful flourish before someone came to clear out her home to make way for someone new? Because, if Fate had any kind of plan up its sleeve, now would be a good time to reveal it.

The main entrance door buzzer sounded, drawing Grace to the entry-phone by the flat's front door.

"Hello?" she answered.

"It's the cavalry."

"Bev! Thank God."

Three

Once another cup of tea had been arranged and enjoyed with the chocolate brownies Bev had brought, the two of them set to work.

"What about the old record player?" Bev wondered. It was sitting on top of the sideboard.

"I'm sure it works," said Grace.

"Perhaps we should test it."

"Okay…"

Aunt Jen had quite a few vinyl records from the old days, so Grace chose a Beatles album, *Rubber Soul* from 1965. It was a bit crackly but that was okay. It was almost as old as she was. It was entitled to be crackly.

"Right, we ought to get started then," she said.

"Definitely," said Bev.

Once they had finished singing along to 'Baby, You Can Drive My Car' and 'Norwegian Wood', they began with the bedroom.

"A challenge," said Bev.

"You're not kidding," said Grace. "I was thinking of placing stuff for charity in black sacks. Anything that looks too tired, we can pile up on the bed."

"Clutter, clutter, clutter…" Bev muttered as she peered into the bottom of the wardrobe. She promptly removed three pairs of unworn slippers, three foldaway umbrellas and six volumes of ledgers that looked straight out of a 1960s office.

"I could do with a spare brolly," said Grace.

"Not sure about these though," said Bev.

She handed the first of the ledgers to Grace, who opened it.

The top of the first page, in bold black handwriting, stated: 'Shawcross Lyric Theatre Bookings.'

"Wow…"

"What is it?" Bev asked.

"Judging by the handwritten entries of dates, production, and performer, it looks like a list of people who appeared at the Lyric a lifetime ago."

Bev squinted at the page. "Interesting."

"Look," said Grace, "the first booking's dated 10th June, 1962. The production: Bill Harris Variety. The performer: The Albert Saxby Quintet. The address, care of The Murray and Wilson Agency, London WC2. I suppose it makes sense – Aunt Jen worked in the Lyric's office for decades, right through the renovation period of the late-90s to the start of the new era. She must have rescued these rather than see them thrown out."

She tried the final volume, to see where it went up to.

"The last entry's September 1982. Most likely the records were put on a computer after that."

"I don't think so," said Bev. "I started at the council a couple of years before that. Our computer back then was the size of a small house and must have cost a fortune. There weren't cheap personal computers like today, and certainly nothing a local theatre could have afforded. I think it's pure nostalgia that saved these."

Bev picked up the first volume and flicked slowly through the pages.

"Look at this. Every few pages, someone's written a comment after a performer's name. Sharon Strand, singer: 'Big head'… Lenny The Laughter Machine Lewis, comedian: 'Not funny'… Colin Randall, juggler: 'Wandering hands'… Coco Vincenza, singer: 'The Unforgettable' – although that's jotted in front of the name… Robbie Stone, magician: 'The police have been informed'…"

"I wonder if there are any famous names," said Grace.

"Bound to be."

Bev handed it to Grace, who hesitated before turning the page again. It struck her as funny how easily she could be dragged into a distraction.

"We don't really have time, Bev."

"You're right."

Bev pulled out the rest of the stuff from the bottom of the wardrobe. There were some rolled-up posters, various leaflets and show bills.

"Wow, this one's Dusty," she said.

"I'll get a damp cloth," said Grace.

"No, Dusty… as in Dusty Springfield. It's an official handout."

She handed the glossy sheet to Grace, who squinted at the scrawl across the promotional photo.

'To Jen, love Dusty Springfield xx.'

Grace smiled. "Aunt Jen must have met her – probably in the early sixties. This would have been before Jen worked there. Obviously a fan."

"When did she start working there then?"

"I'm not sure. A few years later, I expect. I reckon she must have met quite a few stars. She never said much about it though. I mean, she'd mention names occasionally after a Christmas sherry, but she wasn't one to speak of the old days much."

"Dusty Springfield," Bev mused. "Is there anything written on the back?"

Grace turned it over.

"Just the names, venue and date."

"Amazing," said Bev, leaning in for a closer look. "I'll tell you something else too. It looks like the same handwriting as the comments in the ledgers."

"Does it?"

Grace went back to the list of performers in the first volume of records. The comments were indeed in the same hand – her aunt's. The sheer cheekiness of it made her smile, even though it wasn't something Grace herself would have ever done.

"So, she *was* working there that early. She must have been, what, eighteen. It makes sense too. These lists were probably created by someone senior to make sure the right people were admitted at the stage door. Aunt Jen would have checked them in as part of her job."

"This one though…" Bev's finger was pointing at a page where the only name with a comment provoked a question. "Why did she write 'The Unforgettable' in front of Coco Vincenza?"

Grace suddenly had an urge to ask her aunt for details. But that wasn't possible.

"Bev," she said, closing the book, "we have an entire flat to clear. Let's get to it."

Four

Grace peered out from the passenger seat of Bev's Citroen looking for a parking space. They had just pulled into the supermarket car park, which looked pretty full – as it always did late on a Saturday morning.

While Grace did most of her main shopping during the week, Bev had a council admin job and so it was a home delivery of the basics that morning at nine and then out to top up at eleven. Jez, her husband, showed no interest in shopping for groceries and would instead spend the morning watching any sport on TV while leaving comments in the dozens of Facebook groups he belonged to.

"We've been over this before," said Bev in relation to the business of making a difference. "There's nothing wrong with helping in a charity shop. You could go back to it."

Grace had previously volunteered two mornings a week at Heart Sense until it closed down a couple of months back. There were plenty of other establishments, of course.

"Possibly, but I was serious when I said I'd like to do something like Lesley Pearce. I just don't have twenty-six miles in me. Twenty-six yards would be pushing it."

Bev spotted a parking space and pulled into it.

"The thing is," she said, switching the engine off, "we can't all be Lesley Pearce. How about thinking a bit smaller – you know, helping one person, but in a big way."

"You described me as a creature of the background, a non-speaking shepherd… but I've promised to celebrate Aunt Jen's life by getting out there and doing something. That's what motivates me. Well, that and having you denounce me to the patrons of the Sunny Side Up Café. What was it? A miserable fraud?"

"A *pathetic* miserable fraud."

Grace's back and sides twinged as she got out of the car – thanks to all the lifting and shifting activity at her aunt's, which wasn't quite finished yet. She said nothing though as the two of them headed for a long line of trolleys.

"I'm going to do something amazing, Bev."

"I know, but wouldn't it be better to think of something achievable? I mean, isn't there someone you could help in a way that makes an important difference to their life?"

"There must be hundreds of them out there."

"You only need one."

"You're right. I only need one."

A minute or two later, pushing a trolley apiece, they entered the supermarket.

"How would I realistically make a difference in someone's life?" Grace wondered.

"Well, first, you have to choose a victim."

"Bev…"

"Be honest – anyone receiving your help is going to need counselling afterwards."

"I think it's *me* who needs counselling."

"There's a thought. How about trying the psychology guy on South Hams Radio?"

"You're joking."

"Yes, I am. The whole town would hear."

"I could give a false name."

"Changing the subject, how about we look at the clothes?"

"I don't need a new wardrobe, Bev. A new life, maybe…"

"It's a pity you didn't keep the receipt for the old one. You could have returned it for a refund."

"I'm heading for the frozen aisle."

"Okay, the frozen aisle. You win."

Tying up the loose ends in Aunt Jen's flat was making Grace wonder about her own life. It was definitely time for a fresh start, but what would the future hold for an all-new Grace Chapman? It was hard to see the path ahead. Her life so far had been one of playing it safe and staying out of the spotlight. She'd always supported others in their efforts, but as for leading the charge… no, never.

She opened a fridge door and selected an individual chicken pie. Would shopping for one ever feel natural? She placed it in her trolley.

Just then, she spotted something unexpected. It was a tall man helping a shorter woman by reaching up to the spicy pizzas on the top shelf. The woman, she didn't know. But the man…

He lived hundreds of miles away in the North and only came down to Shawcross occasionally to see family and friends. This had to be one of those times. Usually though, he stayed on the other side of town. That's why she'd only caught a glimpse of him fewer than a dozen times in several decades.

She turned to Bev, who had been a few feet behind her – but who had since turned away and was heading out of the aisle.

Grace followed, uncertain of what to say.

"I fancy some fresh halibut," said Bev. "What about you?"

Grace was still undecided.

"Er… chocolate."

Bev turned left at the next aisle, while Grace continued onward and took the fourth aisle on the right. In truth, she didn't need to be there. It was a tactical withdrawal.

Placing a bar of dark orange chocolate into her trolley, she turned… and crashed into another trolley. And now her heart was pounding. Not because of post-crash stress, but because…

He smiled apologetically.

"Sorry, that was my fault. I've got a wonky wheel."

She couldn't speak. "Uh…" Not sensibly, anyway.

"Front left," he added.

"What?" she finally spluttered.

"Hang on," he gasped. "It's Grace… isn't it?"

"Sorry, could you please get out of the way."

"It *is* you," he called as she turned out of the aisle.

Silence seemed to be the best option.

"How's it going?" he continued, which meant he was behind her, speed-stalking… "I mean… how are you?"

She stopped and he drew alongside.

"Grace, I just… it's me, Russ Adams, by the way."

She knew that, of course. She was staring into a face with forty-odd years of life having been etched into it since the last time she'd had a proper look, but he hadn't changed much at all. Despite the mousy brown hair thinning and greying slightly, and the previously smooth skin having gained a line or two, he looked good.

"Sorry, I have to go," she finally said.

"To be fair, it's a bit of a romantic cliché, isn't it. Two long lost friends meet in the supermarket on a Saturday, and by midweek they're… well… friends again."

Grace shook her head. "Let's get one thing straight…"

But Bev suddenly appeared.

"Oh… my… Grace, it's him! The one that got away!"

Grace was incandescent.

"Excuse me, Beverley Sullivan! That was forty-four years ago."

"Wow," said Bev, "and you're almost over it!"

*

Waiting in line at the checkout, Grace was still furious. Bev, with half her shopping list not in her trolley, queued behind her.

"He just said hello, that's all."

"Bev, we called you the school matchmaker. I thought you'd retired from the role."

"What? I don't know what you mean."

Grace rolled her eyes. There was definitely something contrived about all this.

"I wasn't born yesterday," she informed her best friend. "That was a setup."

"No, it wasn't," said Bev.

"Well, only a little one," said Russ, appearing unexpectedly at Bev's shoulder.

"I don't believe it," said Grace.

Russ tried to keep his smile intact but was failing.

"Bev said you were trying to socialize a bit more since your breakup."

"Bev said…? When?"

"We're Facebook friends," said Bev.

"What?" Grace then realised they were providing entertainment for anyone nearby, so she lowered her voice. "Since when?"

"Five or six years," said Bev, also lowering her voice. "Someone posted a photo of our old school and Russ commented. I replied to his comment, and we became friends."

"And you never thought of telling me?"

"Why would I? You'd have called me a traitor – even though almost half a century has passed."

"It's okay," said Russ, in a light-hearted stage whisper. "We don't have to see each other again. I'm staying with my Aunt Ellen for a while, that's all. I only popped in here because…"

"Russ is still teaching music," said Bev, cutting him off. "And he plays piano beautifully. There's some of his stuff online."

"A few modest compositions," said Russ.

"Well, that's lovely," said Grace, feeling that it was of no consequence to her, but recalling how he'd played keyboards in a failed teen band.

"He's helped hundreds of kids find something in themselves," said Bev. "You know, made a real difference."

Russ shrugged it off. "Bev says you're looking for a way to make a difference."

"That was quick. I only told her on Thursday."

Russ smiled warmly. "I remember you in the old days, Grace. You'd work your socks off to help others, but you never came out of the shadows. Even if it was your idea, you'd let others take the lead and take the credit. I think it's great you want to make a difference on your own terms."

"Ah," said Bev, "I think we've changed that to making a *small* difference."

"Excuse me," said Grace. "I need to get some desserts."

And with that, she wheeled her trolley away from the checkout and back into the heart of the store.

She was quietly fuming as she turned into the wrong aisle. She grabbed a pot of spicy salsa anyway and fumed some more.

What did he say? 'It's great you want to make a difference on your own terms'…?

He made her sound like a lightweight. But she wasn't. Her past was full of big tasks being undertaken.

What about her interest in family history? Hadn't she decided to write a book? Yes, she had! It was to be a tome that pulled together the lineage of Olive Marshall, the woman who adopted her as a baby. She once spent an entire Monday on a genealogy website tracking down Olive's great, great, great grandfather, William Hughes of Liverpool. Okay, so five years had passed since then, but it was definitely a project she would revisit at some point, possibly to look up the Taylor connection at the great, great, great, great grandparent level.

Actually… was it Taylor or Naylor?

She steered her trolley towards the dessert aisle and thought of Russ. Yes, he looked good for his age, but so what? She was a serious and sensible person who knew how to avoid having unnecessary drama in her life.

Five

Clutching a toasted cheese sandwich on a plate, Grace sat down on the sofa and exhaled loudly. In her twenties and thirties, she'd had the power to sit down silently. But sometime in her late forties, a little sigh crept in, which had gradually become louder and turned into an 'oof!' over the years. For the life of her, she could think of no purpose it served.

It had been a busy Sunday followed by a hectic Monday morning, but it was done. Her aunt's furniture had gone to a second-hand dealer, while the rest had all been bagged up, with most of it having been distributed either to the dump or a charity shop. All that remained in Grace's possession now was a large plastic storage box of Aunt Jen's things that she couldn't part with, a record player, and some LPs and books.

A few minutes before two o'clock, she was finally about to enjoy lunch while listening to Jamie Doolan on the radio. He was finishing up a half-hour on what to do with your kids during the long summer holidays.

Her mind drifted back in time to her own childhood summer holidays but failed to linger there. For some reason, her thoughts skipped to her first day at 'big school' and the anxious leap from cosy, comfortable junior school into a noisy, bustling, bewildering hive where she knew no-one.

Ah…

She now knew why her thoughts had gone there.

All those years ago, Mum and Aunt Jen had tried to focus her young mind on the exciting potential for making new friends. But dressed in a stiff, oversized new uniform, she'd felt like a prisoner entering jail for the first time. And, as if that hadn't been bad enough, she'd had to haul a shiny black briefcase large enough to conceal a body, but in fact carrying only a fish paste sandwich and a pencil case. Of course, on that momentous day, with all that self-conscious angst to deal with, the boy was there too. And he'd smiled at her nervously, as if relieved to spot a fellow member of the losers' club.

As time passed, she made more friends, including Bev Sullivan. But she and Russ Adams remained on smiling terms for many years to come – in fact, all the way to their final year when, on a sun-soaked afternoon in May, the smiling became something more.

Back in the present, she shook her head. This was self-indulgent nonsense. Russ was a sixty-two-year-old piano-playing music teacher who lived hundreds of miles away in the North.

Her phone pinged.

It was a message from Bev.

'Well…?'

She typed a reply.

'Well, what?'

'My idea!'

'What idea?'

The phone rang. She answered.

"Bev…?"

"You said you wanted to make a difference. You said you'd find someone you could help."

"I'm still working on it."

"Why not help your OTL."

"My what?"

"One true love."

Grace had no time for frivolous baloney.

"We're grown-ups, Bev. There's no such thing as an OTL. In case you hadn't noticed, humans are attuned to accepting a range of suitable partners."

"I know, but I'll tell you what – if I wasn't married…"

"Hey!"

"Hey what? I'm just saying, if I'd never met my lovely, wonderful Jez…"

"If you weren't married, then what?"

"Where do I start? A lovely weekend away in Scotland with yummy Russ, where the weather closes in and we have to spend the whole time in the hotel room, or a City Break in Barcelona where a strike shuts everything down, so we have to spend the whole time in the hotel room, or a week in Monaco where an unexpected sandstorm blows in from Africa…"

"Bev, you *did* meet Jez. Besides, Russ is no great catch. For one thing, he's obsessed with prog rock."

"That was forty-odd years ago!"

"Well… we don't actually know he's left it behind, do we."

"It could be worse. I wish my Jez would leave opera behind. All those high notes set my teeth on edge."

"I like opera."

"Alright, you have Jez and I'll go for Russ."

"You're very lucky to have Jez. He's a good husband."

"I know. Really, I do."

"Count your blessings, Bev."

"You too. It's just as well you're getting your hair done tomorrow. Don't take this the wrong way, but it looked like a bird's nest when Russ crashed into you."

"I've cancelled the appointment. At least, I will do now you've mentioned it."

"Why?"

"Because he'll think I've had it done for him. Now, if you don't mind, I'm sixty-two and I have a date with a toasted cheese sandwich."

"Alright, we'll say no more about it. Bye for now."

"Bye, Bev."

Grace ended the call and stared across the room at nothing in particular. For a moment, she imagined going out with Russ, but her chest immediately tightened. She hadn't 'gone out' with a man since meeting Dennis. That version of her was more than forty years in the past. Time had changed her. The thought of going through all that again made her tense up. From meeting up for drinks to the first kiss and… well, the whole journey. She'd only completed it once, of course, and that journey ended with marriage. No, actually, that journey was still ongoing, pending a divorce. Hence, her being stuck in a semi-detached house on the suburban edge of town, unable to sell it and move on because it was in her husband's name.

She tried putting herself in Bev's shoes… and tried to enjoy Bev's approach to the situation. A weekend in Scotland where the weather closes in…

Her heart speeded up a little.

No!

She shut the fantasy down. A romance with Russ could never go anywhere, and even if it did? Then what? Hadn't she already done the marriage thing? And hadn't her husband cheated on her and left?

She sighed. Three months into their separation, she was crash-landing in slow motion out of her marriage.

Independence? It was an elusive state. Certainly, finding a good job wasn't straightforward. Having tried and failed to landed receptionist jobs with a doctor and a dentist, and not even receiving a reply from a pharmacy and veterinarian, it was plain that her meaningless CV was a problem. As for work that didn't require one, it was a little late in life to start a stressful, tiring, low paid job with terrible hours.

Still, she'd managed to save a bit over the years from the weekly allowance Dennis gave her.

The thing that hurt most was that he'd never wanted children. Grace had always wanted children but agreed to his preference for the sake of their marriage. Had she known he was going to run off later in life, she could have got rid of him early enough to remarry and have the family she had always wanted.

Too late now, of course.

She wondered what he'd think of her wanting to make a difference. Not that his opinion mattered now, but had they still been together, he would have dispensed a dollop of his usual wisdom. "What is wrong with you?" he'd have said. "You'll get yourself all worked up for nothing. You'll never see it through. Leave it to those who have the know-how."

She took a bite of her sandwich and peered into the storage box of Aunt Jen's things by her feet. It contained a lot of personal stuff that couldn't be thrown out or given away.

Sometimes, she felt lost, where her mind wouldn't settle on any one thing. This was such a time. Right now, her thoughts were searching out anything of interest that might distract her away from her failing life. While she waited for something to occur to her, she idly listened to Jamie Doolan on the radio. He was entreating listeners to call in after the news, when his regular Monday afternoon guest, psychologist Dr Dan Shakespeare, would be taking calls.

Her thoughts suddenly latched onto an idea.

"No way," she wheezed.

"Any problems, Dr Dan can help," said Jamie.

"Not happening."

"So, here's the number you need."

"Nope, don't need it."

"4575…"

"Four, five, seven, five," she repeated as she tapped it into her phone.

Six

Would she make the call? Dr Dan was a well-known British Frasier Crane, and she often enjoyed his insightful engagement with callers.

Yes, she would make the call.

But what if he revealed the real problem – that she shied away from fulfilling her true potential because life was easier in the background, away from the spotlight.

Grace felt herself giving up on the idea. It was a familiar sensation.

She went to the kitchen, still holding her phone, and idly removed a cookbook from the windowsill. She'd make a meal. Chilli con carne. She hadn't done that in ages.

Should she make the call?

She opened the book and found the recipe. There was Dennis's biro all over it, upgrading the celebrity chef's method. In the first of eight changes, he'd scrubbed a half teaspoon of salt and replaced it with two teaspoons. He'd also added new ingredients, namely, tomato ketchup, grated cheddar, and onion gravy granules. Not that he'd ever cooked it, or anything else. He'd simply deliver an insight during the meal, and then rise from the table with a huff and make the change in the book there and then, as if she had let him down again.

She put the book back and returned to the sofa. She *would* make the call – and she would reply robustly that she genuinely wanted to prove her worth and make a difference but couldn't because twenty-six miles was too far to run.

No, this call was *not* going to happen. After all, what if anyone she knew heard the call? What would they think?

Perhaps there was a way though. She'd suggested as much to Bev.

"You've always shied away from taking on a big project?" Dr Dan said to her five minutes later.

"There's usually someone who can do it better, who has more experience. I've always been happy to let them do it, you know, to take a back seat. It's just that I'd like to try."

"Do you have any skills you could use, Heather?" Dr Dan asked.

Grace fell silent for a second or two.

Oh… Heather, my fake name.

"No, not as such."

"I'm sure you have many useful skills, but let's take a different approach for a minute. Might you volunteer for something?"

"Well, I did volunteer a couple of mornings a week in a charity shop, but it closed down. This time I thought I might try to achieve something myself. You know, actually do something without handing it over to someone else. I know someone who runs marathons, for example."

"That's a fantastic way to use a personal goal to raise money for others. A total win-win. Do you run?"

"No."

"Right, so… let's look at this another way. Making a difference can also be a small thing."

Grace's spirits sank, in contrast to Dr Dan's rising enthusiasm.

"Heather, I'd say you need to get over the psychological barrier of identifying a worthwhile project and leading it to completion. The best way to do that is to select an achievable objective. For instance, help someone with their shopping or a trip to the library. Basically, choose something simple where you can absolutely take the lead and complete the task."

"Start small. Yes, that makes sense."

"All you need do is find someone you can help. Just make sure there's a specific goal in mind, one this person cannot achieve alone… and help them achieve it. Make a difference that way."

"Yes, alright, I'll give it a try."

"Who knows, you might become someone who helps others because you're good at identifying an issue and coming up with the best way to deal with it."

"Right."

"And Heather, this is important – you might discover that helping others is its own reward. That way, you'll get rid of your 'make a difference' demons in the most commendable way."

Grace barely had a chance to thank him before host Jamie Doolan took over and steered the broadcast to an ad break.

Ending the call, she put her phone down and did some Rocky-style shadow boxing.

"I will do this… nothing will stop me… whichever victim I choose… watch out, here I come. No naming and shaming in the Sunny Side Up Café for me!"

Her phone rang.

It was Bev.

"Was that you?"

"No."

"I thought as much."

"I thought you were at work."

"I'm working from home today – with the radio on. So, what's the plan?"

"I thought I might leave that to Fate."

"Right, well… it might be worth keeping the fake name for when it all goes horribly wrong."

"Thanks for the vote of confidence."

"No problem, Heather."

"Tell me, am I free of your threat? You know where you denounce me to everyone in the café?"

"Grace… I'd never hurt you in public. That said, I know what you could do."

"You do?"

"Yes – get Russ to help you."

"We're not a double act."

"You could be. Maybe someone needs help musically. If you set it up, Russ would do all the work and you'd get the credit."

"I don't know anyone who needs musical help, but thanks for the suggestion, which I've considered and thrown in the ideas dustbin."

"There might be someone in those old theatre bookings."

"I doubt that's a way forward."

"You won't know unless you take a good look. That first volume looked full of possibilities. Well, maybe one or two. You're not taking me seriously, are you."

"No, but I love your daft ideas. How about next time you're free, I buy you lunch?"

"Ooh, I feel something French and expensive coming on."

"Alright, bye-bye for now then."

"Au revoir, cherie."

Grace laughed and ended the call. Who was she kidding though? She wasn't cut out for a one-to-one 'make a difference' encounter. What if it took her further than she was prepared to go? Perhaps she should just volunteer at another charity shop after all. General help, background support – the real backbone of the charity sector.

She sighed and ventured back to Aunt Jen's box. Spurred a little by Bev's enthusiasm, she took out the first of the six volumes. The top of the first page stated: 'Shawcross Lyric Theatre Bookings' and the first entry, dated 10th June, 1962, was the Albert Saxby Quintet.

No, she wouldn't be helping a quintet.

She turned over a few pages… and there she was again.

The Unforgettable Coco Vincenza.

Her phone pinged. It was message from Bev.

'Why don't I come round straight after work and help you choose a victim? What do you say?'

Seven

It was half-past five and the sun was blazing outside. Grace was indoors on the sofa though, waiting for Bev's arrival. The subject of making a difference was still in her mind but, in all honesty, had already begun its inevitable fade. Even the list of names in the Lyric's old ledgers weren't proving to be much help, although it was good to wallow in all that history, imagining who those people were and what they got up to.

She had always been fascinated by other people's lives, perhaps because she'd yet to meet anyone with a less interesting life than herself. Once, she met an elderly lady in the post office who it seemed had lived the most dull and predictable life imaginable, but when Grace sympathized with the poor woman's old-age limp, she smiled at Grace and said she'd done it in her twenties while mountain climbing in the Himalayas.

The doorbell rang.

"Ah good…"

A couple of minutes later, she and Bev were at the dining table, sipping tea and flicking through the old ledgers.

"I'm assuming we won't be mentioning you-know-who," Bev ventured.

For some reason, Grace recalled a moment with Russ just before sunset on a warm September evening forty-four years ago. They were on a bench at the back of the beach, and he had something important to say. The setting was so romantic. Her excitement was off the scale.

"Grace?" Bev prompted. "I said I'm assuming we won't be mentioning you-know-who."

"Forty-four years ago, his last words were, 'I hope it all goes well for you.' Well, it hasn't all gone well."

"We're right to not mention him then. Now, these old books are fascinating. There's a guy here called Big Eric. It says he was a bawdy songsmith. I wonder if he sang the one about a man called Jock, who had…"

"Bev, no."

"Grace, what are we doing? Are you going to run twenty-six miles or take someone to the library?"

"I'd like to drop the whole thing."

"Not make a difference, you mean?"

"I was inspired for a while by Aunt Jen. I think it's worn off."

"Look, why not just pluck a name from these volumes and track them down. Once you find someone not too far away, you'll probably end up buying them tea and cake while they talk about the old days. A few hours, that's all. Find the right one and you'll make a difference."

"Possibly."

Grace stood up and went to the window. It was a lovely outside.

"Let's see," said Bev. "You've got performers from Glasgow, Birmingham, Chester, Leeds, Norwich… ah, here's a local one."

Grace turned. "Who?"

Bev peered at the page. "Coco Vincenza."

"I've seen that one. Aunt Jen added 'The Unforgettable' to her name."

"The address is only a few miles away. It must have been her own address – she probably didn't have an agent."

Grace came and sat down again.

"Is this Fate at work, Bev? Or just another distraction in a life going nowhere?"

Bev shrugged. "There's no harm in looking her up."

"What if Fate's wrong?"

"How do you mean?"

"Well, what if I need to look a bit harder? There must be thousands of names here. Shouldn't I be more thorough?"

"Avoid a decision, you mean?"

"I mean make a list of contenders before I start approaching them."

"I know you, Grace. You'll be halfway through volume two sometime next year with a hundred names, none of which you've spoken to. You'll either never get to the end of the sixth volume or by the time you do, there won't be one person on your list who's contactable without holding a séance."

Grace took possession of the first volume, turned to page one, and ran a finger a little way down.

"The Incredible Geraldo, magician… I'll google him."

A moment later, she shared the disappointing results.

"He must have performed a vanishing act."

She took a sip of tea.

"Martin Rabatini, comedian. I'll try Facebook." It didn't take long to find something. "There's a Jason Rabatini. Should I contact him?"

"No. Martin's probably his ninety-year-old dad. You'll tell Jason that you're going through old theatre acts, and he'll tell you he's not interested in falling for your scam."

"I'll keep looking."

"Why not just pick one and act on it."

"I might be just a few pages away from the Beatles."

"That's not likely. I'm beginning to see the Lyric wasn't a top destination for talent. I get the idea the real stars played elsewhere."

"You're right. I'm more likely to find the Everly Sisters, which is as much use as finding the Beverley Brothers. I'm not going to give up hope just yet though."

Grace thought about her aunt and those far-off days. Yes, she would pursue this. It wasn't as if she had much else on.

"I've found the Bingtones. A beat combo… Paddy Storr, ventriloquist… Elvis Presley, music man! Wow! No, hang on. Bad handwriting. Elvis Priestley, muscle man."

Bev took the volume back from Grace and turned the page.

"What's wrong with this one – the Unforgettable Coco Vincenza? Why don't you track her down?"

"I don't know, Bev. I think I'm barking up the wrong tree."

Bev smiled. "I don't think you are."

"How do you mean?"

"Don't you see? Coco Vincenza's a singer."

"And?"

"Russ Adams is a pianist."

"Well, I can see something might add up there, but not in a good way."

"Grace, the address after her name is a twenty-minute drive away."

An urge rose up. It was a desire to hide the theatre volumes in a cupboard and start something else.

But no.

"Alright. With any luck, she'll need help understanding her utility bill and I'll be there."

"To make a difference?"

"To make a phone call. Or send an email."

"It's decided then?"

"Yes, it's decided," said Grace.

"Right then," said Bev, smiling with relief. "Watch out Coco Vincenza. Grace Chapman is coming for you."

Eight

On a sunny Tuesday morning, Grace brought her midnight blue Polo to a halt in Dupont Way opposite a large detached Swiss chalet-style house set well back from the road.

"Okay, Coco, let's see if you're at home."

She locked the car and crossed the street wondering if she was doing the right thing.

Number 12 looked in great shape with its white walls and black timbers and long, shrub-lined drive on which sat a cherry red electric Audi. Admiring the house from the open gates, something struck Grace as odd. In fact, the more she thought about it, the more it unsettled her.

She looked up and down the street and back to the house… and then down the street again, because it swept round to the left just past the house. Between the bungalows opposite was a view of the sea.

A memory began to filter through.

"I've been here before," she uttered.

She let the disturbing sensation subside a little before walking up the to the front door and ringing the bell.

A cat came to mind.

A cat?

Grace took an involuntary step back. She wasn't sure why. But there was definitely a cat. Or there had been.

"Hello?" said the voice of a woman speaking through the smart doorbell. She was probably miles away at work.

"Oh, hello… I wonder if you could help me. I'm looking for someone who lived at this address a while back. Her name is Coco Vincenza."

"Sorry, we only moved in six months ago. If it's any help, the people who sold it to us were called Livingstone. I think they had the house quite a while. Maybe try the agent who handled the sale – Lewis and Thorne on Upper West Street."

"Right, well, Lewis and Thorne. That's very helpful. Thanks very much."

Grace withdrew.

Before she got to her car though, she spotted an elderly neighbour outside the bungalow opposite putting a single leaf into her green bin. Nosy, but possibly useful.

Grace smiled at her.

"Can I help?" the neighbour asked.

Grace quickly explained her mission to find a singer from the 1960s.

"Coco Vincenza…?"

"Yes, I lost my aunt recently and she thought a lot of Coco. I thought I'd like to track her down and… you know."

"Tell her the news?"

"Yes, that, but also, bearing in mind her age, see if I can be of help in any way."

"Assuming she's alive, you mean?"

"Yes, that too."

"I do seem to recall a singer."

"You do?"

"I moved here with my parents in 1960. I was just a girl at the time, but I'm sure we kept a clipping from the newspaper – seeing as she lived across the street. It was split into flats back then."

"It must have been Coco."

"I think her real name was Mary."

"Oh… right." Grace had a very strange feeling.

"She moved away years ago though. I wouldn't know where she is now."

"You mentioned a clipping?"

It took the neighbour twenty minutes to locate the scrap of newspaper in question.

"Here we are," she announced as she finally reappeared.

The article from 1964 featured a grainy black and white photo of a young woman. The headline said, 'Success Begins At Home'. The story described local girl Coco Vincenza as having a chart hit thanks to her velvety vocals gracing the microphone in front of the Tommy Cranley Big Band. It revealed 'Seize the Day' as the song title.

"Would you mind if I took a photo of it?"

"Be my guest."

Grace took a photo of the clipping with her phone.

"Thanks, that's brilliant."

"Then there's this one."

The neighbour handed over a more recent cutting – one from 2008. It was an article by Roger Halton looking back at the music scene of the early 1960s. One of the interviewees was Coco Vincenza, the singer.

"Interesting…"

"You can take a photo of that one too, if it helps."

Grace did so, thanked her again and returned to her car. Before driving off though, she googled Coco's hit.

There were a couple of offerings mentioning 'Seize the Day' as a Number 40 minor hit by the Tommy Cranley Big Band, who seemed to have had two other minor hits in the late 1950s. There was no credit for Coco Vincenza though, and no links to any video or audio. It was very much a forgotten song by a forgotten artist.

Her phone pinged.

It was a message from Bev.

'Still okay for lunch?'

Grace called her back.

"Guess where I am."

"How many guesses to do I get?"

"I'm outside Coco Vincenza's old house."

"Oh, well done you."

"I've found out her real name too – Mary."

"That's great. Now, are you still okay for lunch, or have you and Mary booked a table at the Ritz?"

"Don't mock. Coco Vincenza was a star. She got a mention in a proper publication."

"Variety magazine? The Stage?"

"The Torbay Echo."

"Well, that's something."

"It is. Most people don't get their name in the Echo unless they've committed multiple burglaries."

"True."

"The only thing is… she doesn't live here anymore."

"Okay, so what about lunch?"

"I'll see you at one, Bev."

"Great. You can tell me all about it."

Grace started the car and pulled away. She only got fifty yards though before she pulled over again. It only took five minutes to get through to the newspaper.

"Hi, I'm researching the pop music scene of the early 1960s and I'm hoping to track down one of your reporters – Roger Halton. I think he might be able to help me."

"Roger? I'm sorry, he moved on quite some time ago."

"Oh right. In 2008, he interviewed Coco Vincenza, the singer."

"Coco Vincenza?"

"Yes." Grace didn't bother to add 'The Unforgettable'. "I was wondering if you had Roger's email address."

"Obviously, I can't share that with you, but I can email him with your details, if you like. He might get back to you."

"That's very kind, thanks."

"I can't promise anything."

"No, I understand."

Twenty minutes later, Grace dropped the car back home and walked the mile down to the shops near the seafront.

Sometimes, especially like now when the sun went in, she sensed a tiredness about Shawcross, as if it were fading. There had once been a bakery on the end of the row across the street. Now it was a fried chicken shack. The hobby crafts shop was now a minimart. And the florist's had become a betting shop. Maybe it was the way of the modern world. Or maybe it just needed freshening up.

The sun came out again and everything looked better.

She checked her watch. It was ten to one. With a little time to kill, she headed down to the sea wall and faced the high tide waves breaking halfway up the beach below.

"At least you never change. Same old sea, rolling in."

Patience. That was the thing. Those waves knew they would eventually turn this place to sand. It might take a million years, but there was no hurry. The waves had a job to do. They had started it, they would finish it, and they wouldn't be handing it over to someone else.

She turned away and crossed the street again. Next stop would be the café and lunch with Bev.

On the way, she thought of Russ Adams. What was the harm in reconnecting just a little? Perhaps she could be bold for once and take charge of the situation. It didn't need to lead anywhere.

Nine

The Sunny Side Up Café was bright and airy with a great lunch menu, friendly staff, and Russ Adams, who was waving at them from a table at the back.

"Bev? Explain?"

"Explain what? Oh look, there Russ!"

"What's going on?"

"Oh, alright. I saw him on Friday night. We had a good chat about the old days, about school, about you, and… well, I just thought…"

"Think again, Bev."

"Right. Will do. I can't make him disappear though."

This wasn't how she wanted it. Yes, a possible friendship with Russ, but this constant silly setting up nonsense was off-putting. She didn't want a reheated relationship with him.

Once they'd ordered their food, they joined Russ. After all, Grace couldn't abide rudeness.

"Hi," he said, smiling warmly.

"Hi to you too," said Grace, now wondering if it was worth them even being friends.

"Um, sorry about the trolly crash. I hope I didn't break anything."

"Only her heart," said Bev, "but that was forty-four years ago, so you're all good."

"Bev mentioned your aunt," said Russ. "I'm sorry to hear you lost her. The last of the old brigade."

"Thanks… she was more than an aunt. More like a second mum."

"Yes, I remember her. You stayed with her after… you know, losing your mum."

"Yes, I lived with Aunt Jen for six years." A memory flared. "In fairness, she liked you."

Russ seemed surprised.

"Did she? She never said."

"You came round quite a few times, calling for me when we were going to the cinema or what-have-you."

"Yes, I remember. I also remember being round there and kissing you in her front room, and her having the foresight to cough before she came in so we could pull apart and act as if nothing was happening."

"She didn't mind us kissing. After all, she knew you well enough to rule a few things out. Serial killer, for example. Drug dealer, burglar, armed robber…"

"Good judge of character by the sound of it. Between your mum and your aunt, they raised a really nice person."

Grace was slightly taken aback.

"Well, that's a funny way of putting it, but thank you."

She couldn't deny that Russ was nice. And she couldn't deny their history. Or her big fat salty tears of frustration and disappointment when he left. He had been a friend from her first day at secondary school, and for that alone she would always be thankful.

While Bev probed him about life as music teacher, Grace pondered a decision. Thanks to a fear of making herself look daft, she had never been bold. But this wasn't likely to turn into some weird summer romance. It would simply be her letting a man from her past back into her life for a short period as a friend.

Wouldn't that be okay?

"Perhaps we could have coffee sometime," she suggested.

"Good idea," he said. "I'd love to."

He smiled and she recalled that time Bev chalked a huge heart on the sea wall with the names Grace and Russ inside it. Okay, so that wouldn't be happening, but she could feel herself opening up to a renewed friendship. It would be brief and perhaps fun. Russ was a teacher, and this was the six-week summer holiday break. He'd be gone before anything meaningful could come of it.

"How's York?" she asked. "Are you settled there for life?"

"I think so. It's been home a long time now."

"And down here? You said you're staying with your Aunt Ellen."

"Yes, she's the only one left of that generation. I lost Mum and Dad."

Grace felt for him. "I'm sorry to hear that, Russ."

A silence took over for a moment or two.

"How's Ellen getting on?" she asked.

"She's good for eighty-five. Do you remember my younger brother?"

"Trevor? Yes, of course. How is he?"

"He's well. A maths teacher, no less. He and his wife, Sharon, usually keep an eye on Ellen but they're away for a fortnight with Tina, their daughter, and the grandchildren. It seemed a good opportunity to spend some time with Ellen."

Grace thought it was a lovely thing to do. She also realised how little she knew of Russ's life and family, having once deemed it essential knowledge.

"So, you're here for a while?" she asked.

"Three weeks, I think. I'm planning to see my brother's family when they get back. It'll be the longest I've spent in Shawcross in years. It's normally just two or three days."

Grace was happy. A few weeks instead of a few days. No time for a meaningful relationship, but time enough to get to know each other again.

Or…

The thought of a fling reared up.

It was a thought that made her feel uncomfortable. She couldn't mess around like a teenager. She was a sensible, mature woman. She did crosswords. She watched daytime quiz shows. Her right knee swelled up if she stood on it for too long.

"Coco Vincenza," she said, changing the subject.

"Pardon me?" said Russ.

"A singer from the early 1960s," said Bev. "Grace has some old ledgers from the Lyric Theatre. Coco's name cropped up in them."

"Imagine what it must have been like," said Grace. "A young singer who gets a chance with the Tommy Cranley Big Band who have already made a bit of a breakthrough. Those bands were always on the radio back then. So, there you are, you record a song… I can only guess what that must have felt like. And then, good grief, you turn your radio on and there's you singing. What a thought. Especially if the DJ is predicting a hit. And it *was* a hit. Top 40. That said, I don't think it got any higher than Number 40. Still, how many of us get to sing on a hit record?"

Bev was frowning. "Grace, you're rambling."

"It was actually an interesting period of transition," said Russ. "Throughout the 30s, 40s and 50s, the big bands played the dance halls and performed on the radio. But during the late-50s - early-60s, pop groups with amplifiers began to take over, and kids started screaming for the Beatles and the Rolling Stones. It sounds like your Coco was breaking into a world with a limited future. I mean it was okay for Frank Sinatra for a few more years, but it was no place for ambitious young talent."

Grace's phone pinged. It was text from Roger Halton inviting her to call him.

"I have to make a call," she said, leaving the table. "It's the newspaper."

Outside, against the noise of tourists and traffic, Roger's first question was, "Who are you?"

Grace almost laughed but quickly galvanized herself and adopted a serious tone.

"Grace Chapman. My aunt worked at the Shawcross Lyric in the 1960s. She died recently and I'm hoping to track down a friend of hers called Mary. Well, Mary had a stage name – Coco Vincenza. I know you wrote a nostalgia piece for the Echo in 2008."

"Okay, just give me a moment…"

The line went quiet leaving Grace to wonder what she would do if and when she met Mary.

"…yes, I have an address, but I'm not permitted to pass it on. Privacy laws and all that."

"Of course, although I'm sure she would want to be informed about her friend's passing…"

"As I say, legally speaking, I can't give you any private details. Besides, she might have moved on since then. Changing the subject completely, if you love the old days, there's a lovely old cinema in Polcombe. Architecturally speaking, there's quite a bit of history all around there. The grand old apartments opposite, for example. I'd be in seventh heaven living there."

"Seventh heaven…?" *Oh! Number seven in the apartments opposite the cinema.* "Thank you, Roger. That's most interesting, historically-speaking."

It was strange being the All-New Grace Chapman on a mission to make a difference. At this point, the Old Grace Chapman would have jotted the address down on a piece of paper and not done anything about it for five years. Then, when it finally occurred to her to get started, she wouldn't have been able to find the piece of paper.

But people can change, which meant she would soon be getting in touch with The Unforgettable Coco Vincenza. It was just that it felt odd – as if she shouldn't do it.

Ten

Number 7, Coronation Way, opposite the old cinema in Polcombe, failed to produce an actual Mary, but the couple living there recalled forwarding mail to Mary Gordon at 22, Woodbury Lodge – a sheltered accommodation block just across town.

Back in the car, Grace googled Woodbury Lodge to discover via a website that it was a large 1980s beige brick building with landscaped gardens. It comprised forty-four apartments for senior citizens, with a red pull cord in every kitchen, bathroom and bedroom, and a duty manager available 24/7 should there be a problem or emergency. There was also a spacious comfortable lounge for meeting other residents and guests, and a large garden with patio furniture.

She then googled the most popular girls' names of the 1940s. Mary was top of the list.

Ten minutes later, she pulled up opposite.

The green space in front looked well cared for, with a neat box hedge defining the perimeter and a church-style lychgate with a slate roof providing access to a footpath up to the main entrance.

Is this complete nuts?

She set the thought aside, went straight up to the main door, and tapped 22 into the keypad. She would find out how she might help Mary… or Coco.

"Hello?" said an elderly woman's voice.

"Hello? Is that Mary Gordon?"

"Yes, who is it?"

Grace explained who she was and that she was bringing sad news of her aunt's passing. Mary fell silent for a moment but agreed to meet Grace in the communal lounge. A buzzer sounded and the door lock mechanism clicked.

The lounge was a vast space with a dozen or so people dotted around it in twos and threes – most likely residents and their visitors. Another dozen or so were outside in the garden.

Grace took a seat by the dormant fireplace and tried not to listen to the nearest conversation.

A moment later, a thin, grey-haired woman of around eighty wearing a colourful 1960s Mary Quant-style dress came in and looked around.

Grace waved. "Mary? I'm Grace. It's lovely to meet you."

Mary seemed a little shaken as she took a seat.

"Poor Jen…" she murmured.

"Did you know her well?" Grace asked.

"Yes, she was an old friend. To be honest, last time she came to see me, she did seem a bit worn out, bless her."

Mary became a little emotional and Grace supposed this wasn't the time to ask about anyone being 'unforgettable'.

"Did you know my mum, Olive?" she asked instead. "She was Aunt Jen's older sister."

Mary took a moment to compose herself.

"Yes, very much so, although it was your aunt I knew best."

A thought, too strong to suppress, came to the fore.

"Did you have a cat?"

Mary looked surprised.

"No."

"I think she was called Tammy."

"No… but… *oh my*. My flat-mate Sandy had a cat called Tammy. That's going back a bit."

"I remember the house."

Mary seemed to struggle with it. But then it came to her.

"Yes, it was a big house split into flats. Sandy went off to Spain with her boyfriend… and I was meant to look after her cat. Only, I got a last-minute booking somewhere. If I'm right, your aunt volunteered to feed Tammy."

"She must have taken me along."

"Yes… well… a blast from the past."

"I must say, Mary, you're the best-attired person I've bumped into today. Where did you get such a great retro dress?"

"Retro? This is an original."

Grace was a little taken aback.

"Oh… it looks very 1960s."

"It *is* very 1960s."

"Well, it's fabulous. I mean the quality…"

"I got it from the wardrobe department of a London stage production. I was meant to return it, but the costume girl switched to another production and… well…"

"Right… anyway, I looked you up, so I know a bit."

Mary gave her a steely-eyed stare.

"Do you?"

Grace fought off a need to escape.

"You had a hit single with the Tommy Cranley Big Band."

Mary's eyes widened. "Actually, they had a hit with me. As Coco Vincenza, I was the main attraction."

"Ah right, I see."

"We were Number 40 for a week. That's a hit."

"Yes, it is. Amazing."

"For a month or so, I was famous. Television, radio, newspapers, magazines… it didn't last though. In some ways, it was the end of an era. There were all these pop groups with electric guitars taking over the dance halls and the pop charts."

"It must have been an interesting time. Can I ask why you changed your name to Coco Vincenza?"

"Does Mary Gordon sound showbiz to you?"

"No, I suppose not."

"And Lizzie La Grange didn't work."

A familiar black and white photo came to mind. One she had seen a thousand times over the decades.

Oh… Lizzie.

Mary Gordon got to her feet.

"Let's go outside."

Eleven

Grace smiled as she followed Mary out to the patio… and beyond, to the far side of an ornamental goldfish pond, where a wooden bench looked inviting.

"My new favourite place," said Mary.

Reaching it, they both sat down with a loud sigh.

"Let's talk about you, Mary."

"Oh… well… my story started a long, long time ago, when dinosaurs roamed the earth. Actually, let me tell you something I discovered. You can't stand still in life. You either move forward or you move back. Maybe you've found that yourself."

"We were talking about you, Mary."

"Are you moving forward, Grace?"

"I'm sure I must be."

"You don't feel life's happening somewhere else?"

"What a strange question." *Yes, I do feel like that.* "No, of course I don't feel like that."

"Do you ever take time to reflect?"

"Yes, I do."

"And what do you reflect on?"

"This and that."

"A deep thinker then."

The need to leave was beginning to intensify.

"I'm no different to most other people. Now, I'm sure we were talking about you."

"Alright then," said Mary, "I miss singing. I really do. There, you wanted to know something about me and now you do. I'd love to sing again."

"I might be able to help you with that. I could get you some karaoke tapes."

"Karaoke?"

"It's taped music minus the vocals. You just sing along with it."

"I know what it is, thank you." Mary turned wistful. "I'm an artist. I only work with real musicians."

"Of course. Sorry." Grace watched as a neon blue dragonfly came to hover above the pond. "I wasn't thinking."

"Oh, don't mind me. You came in person to tell me about Jen. Most people wouldn't bother. Giving a little of your time to others is a lovely trait to have. Your mum would be proud of you."

The dragonfly flew off again.

"She died when I was fifteen."

"I know."

"Of course you do." A thought struck. "I was wondering… what was she like in the old days?"

"Olive? Oh, serious but positive – and very practical."

"Yes, that's her… I still miss her. Before she passed away, she told me she'd never been happier than watching me growing up to be a sensible girl. She told me to 'keep up the good work'. I didn't know I was about to lose her. She never said how serious things were."

"It can't have been easy."

"No… Still, I was lucky. I had Aunt Jen."

Mary smiled.

"Well, it's been lovely to meet you," she said somewhat unexpectedly. "Please feel free to call again. I don't get many visitors."

"Oh, right. Well, I'll leave you to it. Only, I was wondering… is there any way I could help you?"

Mary seemed puzzled. "I'm not sure what you mean."

"You'll laugh, but I've decided I want to make a difference. It's in Aunt Jen's memory. I thought if I could help someone with their shopping or something…"

"Well, that wouldn't make much of a difference for me, personally."

"No… right…"

"I read about a woman who gave her son a kidney. Now, that's making a difference."

"Yes, well, I was trying to find something I could manage. The truth is, there's a woman called Lesley Pearce who runs marathons and raises money for charity. It just seems a bit…"

"Running a marathon's a terrific idea for someone young like you."

"Ah no, I'm actually sixty-two."

"Yes, *young*."

"No, no… I'm not looking to end up in the back of an ambulance. I just thought, while I'm here to talk about my aunt, something might… you know."

"Occur to one of us?"

"That's a bit harsh – but yes. To be honest, I'd love to find a way to raise some real money. You know, to really make a difference."

"Music is my thing. My *only* thing, really. Perhaps I could help you with something in that area?"

"Well, no, it's *me* who's meant to help *you*. Now, I'm not likely to put on a charity show, but…"

"There you go! What a good idea."

"What, putting on a show? Oh no, bad idea."

"No, it's not. The only running you'll do is between the stage and the dressing rooms."

"No, it has chaos written all over it."

"Tell me – how much does your marathon friend raise?"

"Oh… when she runs the London Marathon, it can be a couple of thousand."

"There you go then. You could raise that with a charity fundraising concert. Especially if you went about it in the right way."

"No... I mean... I wouldn't know where to start."

"Think big. Live Aid raised millions."

"Yes, well... perhaps that's thinking *too* big."

"Agreed. You'll arrange something smaller. Good start!"

"I haven't agreed to anything, so let's not get ahead of ourselves."

"Why not?"

"Well... because..."

Grace wondered. What if she borrowed a guitar, learned to play, then the two of them could busk outside the supermarket. If Coco-Mary sang her hit, they might raise a few pounds, possibly.

"We could achieve something," said Mary.

"Hmm... the Unforgettable Coco Vincenza..." Grace mused.

"The what?"

"Your stage name."

"No, I was never that. Just Coco Vincenza."

"Not the unforgettable?"

"No, why would you think that?"

"It's what Aunt Jen wrote next to your name in the old Shawcross Lyric bookings ledger."

"Did she?"

"Yes, she worked there in the 1960s and jotted comments about some of the performers."

"The unforgettable… I must say I like it."

"Do you?"

"Let's go with it. The Unforgettable Coco Vincenza. Yes, I'll be the main attraction for you. No charge."

"Er…" Grace felt a surge of doubt. What was it her husband used to say? She couldn't arrange a booze-up in a brewery. "I'll um… well, I'll look into it."

"Marvellous," said an enthused Mary. "Now, to get things underway, we're going to need a pianist. Do you know anyone?"

Twelve

A couple of days later, Grace and Bev were enjoying a leisurely stroll along the busy, sunny seafront on a lazy route to the Bay View Hotel for lunch. It was one of Bev's days off, so there was no rush.

Despite an upbeat atmosphere all around them, Grace was still struggling with the idea of helping Mary Gordon. No wonder people ran marathons. As long as you avoided a heart attack, the whole thing was incredibly straightforward. Simply get a place on the official list, set up a Just Giving page online, encourage people to sponsor you, run the race, and the charity gets the cash. Easy-Peasy.

"Do you know something, Bev? Up until recently, I was living a perfectly normal life. Now I seem to have entered some kind of crazy world."

Bev laughed. "If this is about making a difference, you've barely got started. In fact, you *haven't* got started."

"Yes, I have. I went to see Coco-Mary for a cup of tea. Next thing I know, she wants me to set up a charity concert."

"Yes, you told me – but you haven't actually done anything about it."

"Nor am I likely to. I'll tell her it can't be done. I'll say there's not enough time or people… or money. Or something."

Grace stopped to look down at the beach… and out to sea. A small boat on the horizon was going somewhere.

"Just get something started," said Bev, stopping alongside her. "Identify the first thing and do it."

"I wish I could."

"Logically, you need a venue. So do that. Hire a venue."

"Are you nuts?"

"No, I'm pointing out your first move."

"Hire a venue? Just like that?"

"Yes, just like that. How about the Lyric, seeing as that's what started all this."

"No, it's the height of summer. It'll be fully booked."

"Book it for the autumn then."

"No, we'd need tourists to come if we wanted to fill it up."

"Then find a way to book it for the summer. You might be able to get a matinee performance arranged."

Grace shook her head. "I just can't see it."

"Then don't go on about making a difference. Just accept you're not that person. Don't forget, there's a ton of daytime TV shows waiting for you to watch them."

"That's not funny."

"Then take Coco shopping or something."

"I tried. She turned me down."

"Grace, there's a part of you that wants to do this. The fear comes from the fact your growth in certain areas is stunted. These are normal coming-of-age fears you're experiencing. Why not get out there and do something amazing, before you have to join Coco in sheltered accommodation."

Grace considered it.

"Yes, alright. I suppose it's true I'm letting fear get in the way."

"That's the spirit. Once you've got the theatre booked, you simply take the next steps."

"What, book a ton of great acts who'll work for free, then charge people money to come and watch it?"

"That's about the size of it."

"Perhaps I should leave it till next summer."

"Hey…!"

"Okay, okay… I'll try this summer."

"Good. Now what about Russ? He'll want to help."

"Russ?"

"Yes, Russ, the musical brains of the outfit."

Grace wondered about that. There was no need to feel awkward.

"Alright, I'll talk to Russ. And I'll try to set up a concert. And if that's a success…"

"You'll release one of those 'We Are The World' singles?"

"No, I'll go home and stay there."

"Honestly, Grace. If you're going to do this, it might be worth giving it everything."

*

They left the seafront and made for Waverley Avenue, where a number of hotels catered for the town's summer visitors. It didn't take long to reach the sizeable Bay View Hotel – a smart six-storey establishment with a large ground floor restaurant and views of the bay from the fourth floor and above. Bev had booked ahead as it tended to get busy with the sheer numbers in Shawcross at the end of July.

Inside, while they waited to be shown to their table, Grace was stunned by a man sitting at a white grand piano on a raised platform in the far corner. He was framed by a couple of potted laurels and seemed to be playing a sloweddown version of Abba's 'Waterloo'.

"That's handy," said Bev. "Just when we need a pianist, we find one playing over there."

They continued to watch as they were shown to their table, which turned out to be situated quite near the piano.

Grace refused to take the bait.

"I haven't been here in years," she said as they took their seats.

"Hey, look," said Bev. "Isn't that Russ?"

"Where?"

"There! Ten feet away!"

"Why are you doing this, Bev?"

Bev's shoulders slumped. "Because it's a strictly limited opportunity to give my best friend a nudge towards happiness. I know I've probably got it completely wrong, but I would've hated myself if I'd let it slip by. Can you imagine you accidentally spotting Russ three weeks from now and then having me say I knew he was in town all along? To be honest, I just thought… seeing as you two were the perfect couple a hundred years ago…"

"Could we change the subject?"

"Not quite. I just want to add that I'm useless and I'm sorry, and that you should give up on me, but probably not give up on Russ."

"You think we were the perfect couple?"

"Yes."

"Hmm… to think we were together for seven years."

Bev sighed. "You were at school with him for seven years. You only started going out with him right at the end."

"Alright, five months then."

"Look back on it fondly, Grace."

Russ ended the Abba piece with a flourish, gave an unnecessary bow, and came over to their table.

"Hello again. Um… I can't stop. I'm playing till two."

He smiled and so did Grace. But why did she have to feel flutters and stirrings?

"You two were great together at school," said Bev.

Grace rolled her eyes. Bev was so brazen. Russ laughed though.

"Grace, let's ignore the lovely Bev. She's right though. Those four months we were together…"

"It was five."

"Was it? Well… I didn't get any university offers near home, so…"

"That's why he went up North," said Bev. "That's where he got an offer."

"I had to take it," said Russ. "I was eighteen and… well, I had a moment of clarity where I could see all the possibilities."

So did I…

"You're right, Russ. We were young. I'm glad it worked out in York."

"I love it up there. It makes sense too. School budgets have been cut all over the country. I'm lucky to be at a school that still employs a full-time music teacher. Look, um, maybe we could speak later?"

Grace smiled and he returned to the piano.

"He'd be a great help with your charity concert."

"How? He lives two hundred miles away."

"He's in town for a few weeks. The whole thing just needs pulling together. I know you can do it."

"I'm not sure. This charity show idea…" But Grace was unexpectedly distracted by the tune coming from the piano. It was pleasant and down-tempo… and…

It was 'How Deep Is Your Love' by the Bee Gees.

Bev laughed.

"Hey, wasn't that yours and Russ's extra-smoochie slow dance song back in the day?"

Grace shrugged.

"He's playing so badly it's hard to tell what it is. It could be the Star Wars theme."

"Wow, you really haven't got over him, have you."

A while later, Russ came over to them at the end of his stint. This time, Bev invited him to take a seat.

"Thanks. I hope my playing didn't put you off your lunch."

"Not at all," said Bev. "Um… we were wondering if you might be able to help with something?"

"Sure. Anything. What is it?"

Bev glanced at Grace, who decided to stay out of it.

"There's a lovely lady called Mary," Bev began. "Under the name Coco Vincenza, she had a pop career in the 1960s, and had a minor hit. Would you be prepared to accompany her on a few songs?"

"Oh right, you mentioned her the other day. Yes, why not."

"Great."

Russ mulled it over. "An old pop star… Bev, you're setting up a lovely thing there."

"No, it's Grace who's setting it up."

Russ looked puzzled. "Is it?"

Bev nodded. "I'm merely drawing the information from her obstinate mind and passing it on."

"Well, tell Grace's mind it sounds fun."

"That's very kind, Russ. I'll pass it on to Grace. She's very keen to make a difference."

"I can tell. It's like she's glowing with an aura of difference-making."

Russ was smiling. It was a moment in which Grace doubted her self-control. If they were friends for a few weeks it would end up going only one way. And for all the fun it might be, the pain of losing him all over again was something she would prefer to avoid.

She stood up.

"I have to go. You guys leave Coco-Mary to me. I'll work something out. Best of luck, Russ. It was good to see you again."

Thirteen

Grace had decided. There would be no further discomfort with Russ. She still wanted to help Mary-Coco in some way though – but how? Hire a different pianist to accompany her on a few songs? What about doing it in the communal lounge at Woodbury Lodge? Would that work?

She walked to the seafront and breathed in the fresh salty air. She was happier already. Indeed, she found herself absently humming a pleasant Bee Gees tune… and then stopped when she realised which Bee Gees tune it was.

There were some young teens messing around as they came up the beach steps. She watched them cross the road. Possibly heading off somewhere to grab some lunch.

It was enough to jog a memory of being fourteen. At school, Russ was quickly becoming a good pianist. She fancied him so she made sure she praised his efforts. He in turn offered to teach her Chopsticks. She laughed and explained that she had two left hands and no rhythm. He offered to play it with her, together. She recalled the 'together' vibe giving her a warm glow – but the teacher came in and ruined the moment.

And now? Obviously the situation was different. Time did that. Forty-plus years was always going to change things.

Except things didn't feel so changed.

She switched the focus. What did Russ want? Was she unfinished business? Was he hoping to get in and out quick? Or was there something more?

He looked good – there could be no argument there. He dressed well too. And what was that a fragrance? Sandalwood and wildflowers? In truth, he was a mature, experienced pianist, teacher and mentor who wouldn't be in town for long.

She peered down into the waves crashing ashore.

How time passes.

Bev strode up and stopped beside her.

"Hi, Grace. Tell me you don't want to see him again, and I'll tell him to stay away while he's in Shawcross."

"I think I want something more than a few weeks of messing around, Bev. It just feels wrong. It's probably me who needs to stay away."

"You know, on a works drinks a while back, I asked some of my fellow old-timers who'd want to be eighteen again. We'd had a few gin and tonics, so it was a raucous 'yes!' followed by everyone then qualifying it by saying they'd take the health and vitality, but actually, not the rest. I mean, all that angst we used to go through… which some of us seem to be going through all over again…"

"I'm fine. Honest."

"I'm not trying to recreate your youth, Grace. I was just hoping you might make the most of what you have now."

"That's the thing. I was never the most confident girl at school. Inside, I'm still not the most confident."

Bev sighed. "Do you think I don't know that? That's why Fate brought us together – for me to always be here to give you a nudge. I am the Nudge Ninja."

"You gave me the nudge towards Dennis."

"Yes, well, I didn't know he had plans for three affairs, including the current one. It's different with Russ though. It's just two mature people having a bit of a catch-up. It doesn't need to go any further unless you want it to."

"Bev, I don't want the high followed by the low. Shall I tell you why? Because the high can only last, what, two and a half weeks? But the low… that would go on for… I'm sure you get the picture."

"Yes, alright, I get the picture. I just thought you and Russ might cheer each other up. You've both come through a tough time. But you're right. We're in our sixties. We've been around long enough to know that suffering in silence is the sensible thing to do."

"I wish you were completely and utterly wrong for once, Bev."

"Me too. Now, what's happening with Mary-Coco."

"Not a lot. She's no doubt waiting to hear from me with news of progress. She's in need of a piano player."

"Oh, that's a shame," said Bev, "Because we don't know any. No, hang on, wasn't there a guy from our distant past…?"

"Yes, well… while I have absolutely *no* interest in a fling with twinkle-fingers, I do see that he's the ideal person to help me make a difference. I wish I'd never started the stupid thing, but the thought of letting an elderly lady down is too depressing for words."

"So, you'll set something up with Russ?"

"Yes, Russ is hired – but strictly as a pianist."

"Great. And would this be at Mary's flat or in a concert hall…?"

Fourteen

On the first day of August, under a powder blue sky, Grace took Mary Gordon to a café near Woodbury Lodge for coffee and a pastry. Mary reacted immediately to the café's bright, bold colours and potted plants, describing it as lovely and a real tonic.

Grace smiled although she thought the café seemed quite average.

"I don't get out much," Mary explained, as if reading Grace's mind. "Still, that's not such a bad thing. The pace of life over the past few years has rocketed."

Grace nodded. The pace of life over the past few *days* had rocketed too.

"Well, Mary," she said once they were seated with their drinks and treats. "I'm hoping we can capture something of your past glories with a concert."

Mary paused, mid-sip.

"What, you're going ahead? I wasn't sure you would."

"I decided yesterday. All or nothing. I'm hoping to put together a number of performers and raise enough money to make a difference."

"I have every confidence in you. And now that there's a performance coming up, please call me Coco."

Grace enjoyed seeing the fire in Mary's eyes.

"Coco then. Maybe you could tell me a bit more about yourself."

"Yes, but first, can I ask *you* something? Are you with anyone at the moment?"

"No. My husband and I are divorcing."

"Ah right. Well, you're still young. Plenty of gas in the tank. You'll have no trouble starting again."

"I'm sure I've mentioned my age before."

"Listen to me. I'm not far off twenty years older than you and I haven't given up. Neither should you."

"I didn't say I'd given up."

"Good, because when he comes along, you'll know."

"When who comes along?"

"Him, the man, the guy, the chap, the bloke, the fellow… the one you're going to fall for. You'll know as soon as you set eyes on him."

"Love at first sight?"

"No, it's more a first sight of someone you'll quickly be open to the idea of loving. If I've learned anything, I've learned that."

"I'm not sure another relationship is what I need right now. Or anytime, really. I don't need the drama. I'll keep my freedom instead."

"Hey, that would make a good lyric."

"It's hardly 'My Way'…"

Coco smiled. "Love isn't always straightforward. That's why there are millions of songs about it."

Grace shrugged. "Did you ever have a relationship that didn't work out?"

"Did I!! Let me tell you – during my heyday… you're not easily shocked, are you?"

"Er…"

"Oh, you are. Alright, I'll keep it clean. The thing is I might have snared one of the lovely, talented Beatles or Stones, but no – back in 1964, I, Coco Vincenza was at the Playhouse Theatre on the Embankment at Charing Cross, where the famous bandleader Joe Loss and his orchestra did a lunchtime show for the BBC. Anyway, Joe liked to have a couple of guest bands, and one day I was the singer in one of them. As fate would have it, I was won over by Dirk Biggs, the drummer in the other guest band, the Farm Boys, a comedy folk outfit from Norwich. They had a single out at the time, 'The Cow Who Became a Mooooooovie Star'. It wasn't a hit. Anyway, by the time he ditched me, my time in the spotlight was already over."

Grace smiled sympathetically.

"But that didn't stop you from trying again?"

"No, of course not! Just as having a hit song a lifetime ago doesn't stop me wanting to perform again. If you want my advice, *Carpe Diem* – seize the day. Although, I admit it's a bit late now. That was the name of my hit, by the way."

"Seize The Day – yes, I know."

"Well then. There you go."

Coco had a need. She'd like to perform again. Was Grace there to help her with that or was she there to waste everyone's time by starting something she couldn't finish? In truth, she still felt a little off balance.

"Look… the concert… I'm going to do my best."

"Just tell me the plan."

"Okay… it's not fully formed yet, but I'm going to try to book the Shawcross Lyric Theatre."

"Good, that's a start. When are you hoping to book it for?"

"I don't know yet."

"Well, don't hang around. I'm not getting any younger."

"Look, you had a wonderful time in the 1960s. You sang, you appeared on TV and radio, you had a hit, and you had a fling with Bert Diggs."

"Dirk Biggs."

"Yes, him. This time, if I can put it together, it'll just be a local event raising money for charity."

"That's fine, Grace. I'm not asking to appear on prime-time television. It's just that after all I've been through, please don't get my hopes up for nothing."

"Don't you worry, I'm going to see this through."
Somehow…

*

After their coffee, Grace drove Coco to the local seafront where, thanks to the pleasant weather, they were able to sit awhile. There was no sea wall like in Shawcross. Polcombe's benches were situated on a strip of green overlooking the bay as far as the eye could see.

There was a distant ship. It looked like a cruise liner. Perhaps if she stood on the bench and waved both arms, they might come and rescue her.

"You've never heard me sing, have you," Coco mused beneath a pink and white striped beany hat.

"No, I haven't."

"Then hear me sing and you'll be manacled to the project come what may."

"I *am* manacled to the project. There's no need to doubt me."

"I don't doubt you. It's just that there are degrees of enthusiasm and degrees of uncertainty. I just feel if you heard me sing, it might strengthen your resolve."

Grace sighed. Having failings was one thing. Having those failings spoil someone else's day wasn't fair.

"Go on then."

Coco gasped. "What here? Are you nuts? Find me a player. I don't mind what kind. Guitar, piano, tin whistle. Then find us a practice space with friendly acoustics."

Grace stared out to sea because that's where Fate was hovering and laughing. Regardless of what she did – wasn't this always going to be a hopeless distraction that came to an unsatisfactory end?

"I nearly toured Britain," Coco said, more softly.

"Nearly?"

"There was talk of a full orchestra and what-have-you, but the follow-up single flopped."

"Right."

"You'll never know the true meaning of emotional pain until you've been a one-hit wonder."

"I'm sure that's an exaggeration."

"Every successful act has an album called 'Greatest Hits'. Can you imagine trying to launch 'Coco Vincenza's Greatest Hit'…?"

"I take your point, although wouldn't it be called 'Coco Vincenza's Only Hit'…?"

"Hey!"

"Remember, the sole aim here is to hold a charity fundraising performance at a local theatre."

"I'm ready when you are."

Grace puffed out her cheeks. How long exactly could she remain in the early stages of making a difference without entering the phase where she had to do something?

"Alright, Coco. Leave it with me."

"We'll need a name. You know like Red Nose Day."

"I hadn't thought of that. What about… the Nostalgia Concert."

Coco shook her head. "You won't get anyone under sixty attending."

"Alright… well, there'll be singing… and we're trying to bring people together. The Harmony Festival?"

"Hey, that's perfect."

"Is it?"

"Yes."

"Good. We've made a start then."

"So, just to be certain… you're really going to do it, are you?"

"Yes, I am, Coco."

God help me.

Fifteen

Under the bright afternoon sun, Grace was heading to the theatre with the intention of booking the hall for the concert. She wasn't confident of success, but she hadn't wanted to phone or email them. This needed the personal touch.

On the way down to the Shawcross seafront, where the Lyric stood, she imagined what a successful show might look like. The acts, the music, Coco in full voice, the applause, the money raised, handing over one of those oversized cheques to the charity, the photo appearing in the local paper... in short, total perfection.

She had no experience of that kind of thing though. How would she get the acts she required? Would she need to invite potential performers to an audition? How would she know who was up to the job and who wasn't?

There was the other factor – according to their website, the Lyric seated 520 people. Could she sell that many tickets? If so, at what price? A tenner? Twenty? Fifty?

Obviously, Russ would need to play a role. Preferably, one of those roles where he made all the musical decisions, because the alternative would be a dog's breakfast.

It was just as well she was meeting him there.

She wouldn't leave it *all* to Russ though, even if she knew nothing about setting up an event such as this. It was simply a matter of finding the best way forward, such as asking someone with experience to lend a hand with some of the event's non-musical aspects. Someone such as Russ, for example, who, according to Bev, had experience of arranging Christmas concerts at his school and taking groups of junior musicians to community venues.

It would certainly be good to spend some time with him, mainly to discuss the event, but also to reminisce about their schooldays… and yes, to talk about his time at university and him getting into teaching. They would be old friends having a catch-up. That was probably the best way forward. And yet, she knew there would be an undercurrent. How could there not be.

She wondered – what was the difference between old feelings coming back to haunt her and new feelings from the here and now? Or were both types about to join forces to trap her in a pincer movement?

Whatever, she was absolutely clear in her mind that she didn't want a romance or a relationship… but perhaps not as clear in her heart. Would it be so terrible having him in her life as much as possible for another couple of weeks?

She considered it. Having Russ in her life for a while… and where it might take her… and ultimately leave her. What a hangover that would be!

"Hi," he called as she approached the Lyric. He was waiting by the main entrance as she'd requested.

"Hi," she called back.

He looked casual but also like a man who knew how to shop for clothes. Her own clothes shopping was always overly evaluated – to the point of mostly not buying anything. As for the Lyric, it was best not observed too closely – or from any distance really. The renovation work of the late-1990s had included a sideways expansion in concrete, with which the original 1920s theatre seemed wholly ill-at-ease.

"Where's Coco?" Russ asked as she joined him by the open doors.

"I didn't invite her. I was thinking this is a task I need to undertake by myself, kind of thing."

"Yes, but surely she's the bait."

"The bait?" Grace felt her brain trying to get to grips with Russ's appraisal of the situation.

"Coco's a star. She's had a hit single."

"Right, and you think that would help us."

"Grace, it elevates your approach from amateur to professional. At least it should do."

"I never claimed to be a professional. I'm just an ordinary citizen trying to do my best."

"That's not who theatres deal with."

"Well, it's a bit late now."

"I'm only trying to help."

"Pointing out people's shortcomings is not helpful."

"Hello," said a woman standing a few feet away in the foyer. Her lapel badge said Judy Frost, Manager.

"Oh, hello," said Grace. "We're the Harmony Festival."

"I see," said Judy. "How can I help?"

"I'm looking to put on a charity concert," said Grace. "I have a star performer who's had a hit single."

Judy eyed Russ.

"No, not him," said Grace. "It's an elderly lady who lives in sheltered accommodation. I'm incredibly proud to have her on board."

"Marvellous, I'd love to meet her. Will she be joining us?"

"No," said Russ, "she's busy with another engagement."

"Of course."

"So," said Grace, "this is what we're thinking…"

"Come to the office," said Judy. "We can talk there over coffee. Have you been to the Lyric before?"

"Yes, many times," said Grace, accepting that the ugly concrete side extension enabled generous spaces within, including educational facilities, a chamber music space, a bar, the Sea View Café, and the outside terrace with the said sea view.

A few minutes later, seated in an upstairs sea view office and appreciating the aroma of piping hot fresh coffee, Grace began to explain the charity concert idea – at which point she hit a buffer.

"Two weeks from now?" said Judy, repeating Grace's preferred booking date.

"Yes, we need to put the show on while there are thousands of tourists in town looking for something to do."

"We could stretch it to three," said Russ. "I don't mind delaying my return home."

Grace was warmed by the gesture, but Judy wasn't moved.

"The thing is we're booked up all summer. Until late September, in fact."

Grace looked a little lost. She turned to Russ for support, not that she expected anything tangible.

"Aunt Jen," he said.

"Ah… yes…" Grace turned back to Judy. "The Lyric is where my aunt worked for forty years. Jennifer Moore."

"Jennifer Moore…?"

"She was here from the 1960s and all through the renovation period to the start of the new era. She retired about twenty years ago and passed away recently."

"Ah, right… I'm sorry to hear that. It's before my time, but my boss, Tony, would have known her. He's been here since the 80s."

"Could we talk to him?" A thought popped into Grace's head. "The concert is in my aunt's memory."

"I see…"

"You must have space. Lunchtimes, perhaps?"

Judy checked something on her computer screen.

"There's potentially a slot on a Monday, three weeks from now. You'd have to speak to Tony but… basically, it's a Monday daytime that's set aside for deep cleaning. If you could start early and finish early, say twelve till one-thirty, then we could clean a little less deeply either side of it. How does that sound?"

Grace almost whooped but restrained herself.

"Thank you. We'll take it."

Sixteen

Late on Saturday morning, Grace was at home, flicking through the first volume of the theatre booking ledgers to pass the time while she waited for Bev. She hadn't needed any shopping so left Bev to her own devices. They would meet for lunch instead.

A 1965 entry caught her eye.

The Rag Dolls, a vocal group.

Grace googled them and found a reference in a blog about the British answer to the Ronettes and the Supremes. The name Suzanne Dawson came up as the lead singer who nowadays painted rustic and coastal scenes in North Cornwall. It didn't take long to find a website and there was Suzanne, a cheery eighty-plus artist. The 'About' section told of her early days as a singer. She gave up the music business in 1967 when she married a music journalist and had two children. The love of painting had always been there though, and so she still dabbled.

Grace thought Suzanne's dabbling was a triumph.

She next used the 'Contact' page to leave a message explaining that there would be a charity concert in Shawcross in three weeks' time. Would Suzanne be interested in attending as a VIP guest?

On a whim, she switched to the third ledger. Almost right away, she found a cabaret singer called Felicity Berlin who appeared at the Lyric in 1973. Grace could easily imagine someone with bright eyes wearing a glitzy black dress like Liza Minelli in the movie, *Cabaret*.

It didn't take long to find her on Facebook. The limited biography available simply said, 'Mother, Wife, Singer.'

Grace sent her a message a moment before Bev's car pulled up outside.

The two friends hugged as Grace emerged into the bright sunlight and they soon set off on foot for their fitness walk to the seafront.

"I'm proud of you, Grace."

"To be honest, I felt a little out of my depth. Russ was supportive though and once I'd paid a deposit we had the first step behind us."

"Did you pay the deposit out of your own money?"

"Yes, I used my debit card. Why?"

"You'll need to keep accounts. All incomings and outgoings. Even if people offer services for free, you must keep a record in case you're asked questions later."

"By who?"

"The tax monster."

"Oh… I didn't think of that."

"You're not a registered charity. You're just an ordinary individual who's raising some funds for a charity. Your records will separate you from the scam artists out there."

"Proper records then. I wonder *who* I could ask to take charge of that?"

Bev rolled her eyes. "Yes, alright, I'll take care of the accounts."

Grace felt good. Things were happening.

The two of them were heading once more for lunch at the Bay View Hotel – this time via the park with its abundant summertime floral displays.

As they strolled briskly through, Grace felt something. Perhaps it was a sense of being in the foothills of achieving something amazing. She was a woman in motion, with a newfound determination, and failure wasn't on the menu – after all, you couldn't fail unless you gave up.

Bev piped up.

"How's it going with Russ? I mean outside of him supporting the concert."

"We're fine."

"Is that all? Not many of us get to restart a coming-of-age romance in our sixties. All that intensity…"

"Don't be daft."

"You took a break, that's all. Now you're picking up where you left off."

"Russ and I are too old for a coming-of-age romance."

"Says who? Don't tell me there's a law against it."

"Bev…"

"It's ageism, that's what it is. Well, we'll fight it, Grace. You and Russ can snog in the corner while I fend off the offended."

"Stop messing about and be serious for once. I came of age some considerable time ago."

"How about a pretend coming-of-age romance then?"

"That's beyond nuts. I mean how would that even work?"

"Think about it," Bev enthused. "No, *don't* think about. Just do it. Reconnect with all the passion you had, pick up where you left off, and see what happens now you're both adults."

"I'm still technically married."

"Yeah, to a guy who's currently busy having fun with someone else."

"The paperwork isn't done yet."

"You're not holding out hope, are you? You were a dutiful partner for decades, while he's had at least three affairs."

"It just feels right to wait for the paperwork to be completed."

"So, you can say you never strayed? Alright, so we both know you're a loyal and dignified woman – one of the best, in fact. There's no law that says you can't be serious friends with Russ though."

Grace came to a halt.

"I'm worried about getting too close."

"You do have feelings for him then," said Bev, stopping beside her.

"I don't know."

"Of course you know."

Grace thought of Coco-Mary talking about *knowing*.

They resumed their walk.

"It might've been easier if he'd never come back."

"Look, it's up to you. Either treat him like a business colleague or have a slightly delayed coming-of-age romance with him. As long as you're happy with the choice you make."

"Bev…"

"Yes, you're a sensible senior – but Russ is a good guy, and he's going back up North soon. The time is now." Bev checked her watch. "Alright, the time is twenty minutes away. We're not meeting him until one o'clock."

"I still can't think why he plays piano there. It's not like he needs the money. Unless his aunt is charging him summer holiday rates for his room."

"I told you – it's a favour for a friend from their time all those years ago at St Patrick's Boys' Club."

"No, you didn't tell me."

"Didn't I?"

Grace frowned. "What kind of friend needs someone to play piano at a hotel?"

"Oh, just a piano-loving friend."

They left the park behind and reached the busy Waverley Avenue, home to the Bay View Hotel.

"All this making a difference stuff," said Bev. "Have you considered looking at it the other way round?"

"How do you mean?"

"Well, what if you let someone make a difference in *your* life?"

"That's an interesting thought. Are you suggesting Russ might be just the person to do it?"

"Yes, and I'm suggesting three weeks is plenty of time."

"You mean a fling."

"I mean a *start*."

"Basically, you're suggesting I throw myself at him."

"No, I'm suggesting we have lunch first. *Then* you can throw yourself at him."

Seventeen

As before, Russ was stationed on a raised platform in the far corner framed by a couple of potted plants. And, as before, they watched while waiting to be shown to their table, which again was situated near the piano. Grace didn't know the song but thought it might be one of Billy Joel's.

"I still say this is a strange booking for him," she said.

"I told you – it's just a favour for a friend. Stop going on about it."

"Why are you doing this, Bev?"

"Because I can see what you can't. Or won't. You both have it. The love sickness. Forty-four years, and you're both still suffering."

"Next, you're going to tell me there's no cure."

"Oh, there's a cure. You know that too."

"I'm going to hire him to accompany Coco. He'll also help point out who's reliable enough to join the line-up. That's it."

Just then, Russ finished the song and came to their table.

"Hi – I can take a two-minute break."

"Great," said Bev. "Take a seat."

"I'd better not. It might send the wrong signal to the manager. How's Live Aid going? Er... Bev mentioned it."

Grace gave him a professional smile. "Russ, will you play for Coco? She'll want to perform her hit."

"Ooh, very businesslike. Okay, I charge forty pounds per hour."

"What?"

"How many hours will you need me?"

"I assumed you'd do it for free."

"I would for a friend."

Grace tried to calm her mind.

"We *are* friends."

"Great – then I'm all yours for free."

"Thanks. And sorry. I think I'm starting to feel the pressure."

"That's alright. It's going to get a lot worse. Just be aware of it."

"I will."

"For what it's worth, you're doing a great job. Not everyone can make a difference at this level."

Grace grimaced.

"I just hope I don't make a complete mess of it."

"Speaking of your life in York," said Bev. She was eyeing Russ. "Didn't you say you live alone?"

Russ raised an eyebrow. "Yes, Bev… *as I told you*, Yvette and I split up ten years ago." He turned to Grace. "No blame. Yvette wanted to travel and do stuff and she found someone likeminded. In the end, I didn't want to hold her back. I realised that a relationship is about making the other person happy, not about trapping them."

"Have you met anyone since?" said Bev.

"I'm probably getting a bit old for that."

Grace nodded. She and Russ seemed to be on the same page. Her husband had cheated on her, as had her dad cheated on her mum before he left for good. Why look for more trouble?

"It hurts when it goes wrong," she said.

"It does," Russ agreed.

In that moment, Grace was ninety-nine percent certain they were both right about not looking to start a new relationship in later life. As for the other one percent… that was best ignored in case it caused trouble. Right now, they were friends. That was enough.

"So, Coco Vincenza," said Russ.

Grace was glad of the shift in focus.

"Yes, a random name in a series of ledgers listing those who performed at the Lyric between 1962 and 1982."

"I seem to recall your Aunt Jen working there."

"She was the one who rescued the ledgers."

Russ seemed to consider it.

"Out of interest, how many names are there?"

"Well, it's six volumes…" Grace hadn't thought of a number. "Must be thousands."

"So why pick Coco Vincenza?"

"Because she's unforgettable. At least that's what my aunt pencilled next to her name."

"Okay, so why would she write that?"

"I've no idea, but Coco doesn't live far from here. There were others but they weren't local."

"Fair enough. Anyway, it's lovely chatting, but I ought to…" He glanced back at the piano.

"Do you enjoy playing here?" Grace asked.

"Yes, it's relaxing. And Bev might have mentioned I know the manager, Terry Price, an old friend from St Patrick's Boys' Club."

"It's nice to do friends a favour," said Grace.

"It's a bit more than a favour. It's actually in exchange for a staff room he's letting me have starting tonight. My aunt's place is great but it's her home."

"So, you've got a hotel room?" said Grace, sensing a potentially dangerous development.

"Yes, it's handy too, being in the middle of town."

"So, teaching," said Bev. "Do you still love the job?"

"Yes, I do, but… that's to say, yes, I love it, but it's wearing me out. I used to teach kids to play 'Chopsticks', but if I hear it now, I get a panic attack."

"Chopsticks?" said Grace. "That's the only thing I can play on a piano. Badly, of course."

"I'll take your word for it. Um… I'd better get back to my duties."

They watched him return to the piano, where he resumed playing with a slow tune by Elton John.

"A hotel room?" said Grace.

"Yes, it sounds quite convenient, doesn't it," said Bev.

"Did you know?"

"Hand on heart, I had no idea. You have to admit though – it's an interesting turn of events."

"Bev, he was staying at his aunt's place, and I was thinking of seeing him there. Do you know why? Because we'd have his aunt there, making us tea and offering us cakes. But now, he has a hotel room."

"Honestly, Grace, there's nothing to worry about. You can quite easily order tea and cakes from Room Service."

Eighteen

It was Monday morning and Grace was driving to Waverley Avenue thinking about how to put a show together. The standard model seemed to be the fundraisers she'd seen on television over the years, which meant music and comedy. For a moment, she imagined the big names stepping onto the stage at the Lyric.

Outside the Bay View Hotel, she brought the Polo to a halt. Russ was waiting for her and stepped up to the car.

"I'll just put this in the boot," he called.

He was holding a long, heavy-looking sports bag.

"What is it?" she called through the open window.

"A portable keyboard. It folds in half."

"That's impressive."

When he said he had something portable, she'd assumed some kind of small children's instrument.

A few moments later, with the keyboard safely stored in the boot, Russ was sitting beside her.

"A you a fan of the piano?" he asked as she pulled away.

"I do like piano music. I've got a good one on CD. Variations on Chopsticks."

"No…!!"

"Just kidding. No, all kinds. Mozart, Schubert…"

"Grace… you rarely make jokes. Can I assume we're now old friends who are completely relaxed in each other's company?"

"You can."

"Great. Perhaps I could teach you a couple of pieces."

"Possibly. We'll see."

"You can get a decent portable keyboard for a couple of hundred."

"Um… I think we've jumped ahead of ourselves."

"I'm serious. They're great to play and if you give up after a couple of weeks, it easily fits in the back of a wardrobe."

"Russ…"

"Sorry, just kidding."

"Let's keep our focus on Coco for now. We need to work out if she's going to be our star attraction."

"Does she know we have history?"

"I mentioned on the phone that we were at school together."

"Right... I'm glad your aunt saved those old books. It's nice."

"Yes, it is."

Grace thought of the names in the books; all gone from the entertainment business now. And then it struck her. Whether the likes of Suzanne Dawson and Felicity Berlin would attend as VIP guests was one thing. But what about whipping up some showbiz magic by having theatre veterans recount a memory of the old days before the host introduced the next act? Would that add some depth to proceedings? Or would it slow things down for a holiday crowd? Once again, her lack of experience bothered her.

"Have you thought about other performers?" Russ asked.

"Yes, I'm wondering if you could help me there. Didn't you have a band at school?"

Russ almost gasped. "You have *got* to be joking..."

"Not this time, no."

Russ shook his head a little but gave in.

"I'll look into it."

"Tell them they'll be needed to do eight sing-along songs in half an hour."

"You've really thought about it, haven't you."

"You'll do a half-hour of piano with different singers."

"Right, okay."

"And we'll have four comedians. Three of them will do a five-minute spot, then we'll have another one as our

Master of Ceremonies. By the time the MC links everything together, we should have a ninety-minute show."

"Right. Great."

The interior of the car fell silent, so Grace switched the radio on. Some romantic orchestral music was playing.

For some reason, she recalled a moment forty-four years ago, when she and Russ were eighteen. It was around half-nine on a late-September evening. They were sitting on a bench at the back of the beach and, like now, had fallen silent. On that occasion, it was because they both knew he had something important to say, something exciting, something she was ready to say yes to. When Grace was fifteen, her mum warned her to keep away from the woods above the far end of the beach. But three years on, in that vital moment, Grace had felt drawn to going there with her man. His big announcement though? It was to say he was leaving Shawcross and going to the Royal Northern College of Music in Manchester. In that single moment, for a fraction of a second, she'd tried to understand how it would fit in with them getting married. Even now, she could recall the conversation...

"Manchester? That's two hundred miles away!"

"Two hundred and fifty."

"I thought you were going to study music nearer to home."

"I had to try for the best course I could get on – and Manchester's where my dad studied. It's where he was born. I know I said I'd try to find something more local, but Manchester's right for me. For my future."

"What about *our* future?"

"We're too young for that kind of thing."

"I was about to let you… borrow my favourite records."

"I know. Now someone else will get to play them. Someone who deserves to."

"But I love… the idea of you playing them."

"I have to go, Grace. I should have been home ages ago. I need to pack my things. I'm leaving in the morning."

She recalled walking home in shock, stung by his plans. And she remembered telling herself, through big salty tears, that by the time she was *really* grown up, say twenty-one, she would have put Russ Adams out of her thoughts so entirely she wouldn't even remember his name.

Nineteen

Grace brought the car to a halt opposite Woodbury Lodge. A moment later, she and a keyboard-hauling Russ were at the main entrance.

"Silly question," said Russ, "but do we have the sheet music for Coco's hit?"

"No idea."

Mary welcomed them over the entry-phone and buzzed them in. A minute or so later, she greeted them at her door and ushered them into a neat and tidy, if small, modern flat.

"Let's get this done," she said.

"Do you have the music?" Russ asked.

"You'd think I would, wouldn't you."

Mary indicated two boxes of stuff spread out on the dining table.

"I was looking for it, but no luck. Then I got distracted."

It reminded Grace of Aunt Jen's stuff.

Russ meanwhile picked up a photo-booth strip of four photos from the table. A young woman and young man were making faces at the camera.

"Early sixties," said Mary. "Taken in London somewhere. He was a funny guy, but he went back to America. What about you two? Any silly pics?"

"No," said Grace.

"Actually, yes," said Russ.

Grace was surprised.

"Long lost now," Russ added. "They went with all the stuff I left behind at my parents."

Then she recalled it. They were sixteen. Bev was there too, along with six or seven others from school on a daytrip. There must have been a photo booth somewhere along the way. They all squeezed in. And then, as everyone was moving on, Russ produced a few coins and suggested one more session. It was just the two of them. How could she have let that memory slip away? It was so strong now. So vivid and vital. She was a little devastated that the photos were lost.

"So, the music…?" Russ wondered.

Mary shrugged.

"Could you hum it?" Grace suggested.

"The vocal part, yes," said Mary. "But that's not the music. That would be vocalist and music copying each other note for note. A great song demands that the vocals and the score are a marriage of fully compatible individuals, blending beautifully to create magic."

Russ smiled. "Mary's right. I could probably work out a backing track to the vocal, but the original arrangement might have a few interesting or even unguessable patterns."

"You must think I'm a fool," said Mary.

"We absolutely do not," said Russ. "Everyone misplaces something sometime. I can't even remember what I've mislaid. There must be whole shedloads of things I've lost track of."

Grace studied Russ being kind and patient with the Unforgettable Coco Vincenza. It made her smile. Then a thought struck.

"Your hit… is it similar to anything?"

Mary stared at her, possibly straining to think of something.

"At a stretch, it's a bit like 'Moon River'. Play that."

Russ made some space on the table and set up his keyboard.

"Without the music to Moon River, we're only a little bit further forward. However…"

Russ played something that sounded familiar. Yes… 'Moon River'… she recognized it and hoped it might help them.

"Yes," said Mary, "but change that bit. Try a lower note… No, lower… now change the next note… higher… higher… play that again…"

To Grace, it now sounded less appealing.

"Are we getting there?" Russ wondered.

"A little quicker... and a lower key..."

Russ had to think for a minute before continuing.

"How's this?"

"Not too bad."

"Is it like your song?" Grace asked.

"No, it's nothing like it. Hang on, I'll record it on my phone."

"What for?"

"It could be our new single."

Grace and Russ exchanged a look of surprise, which become more exaggerated when Mary, or perhaps Coco began singing.

"Tins of beans, and cola drinks, a can of beer and thick pasta sauce..." She stopped. "It has promise."

"It sounded like a shopping list," said a puzzled Grace.

"It's a placeholder lyric," said Mary. "Did you know Paul McCartney's 'Yesterday' was initially called 'Scrambled Eggs'?"

Russ laughed. And then, from memory, he sang a little of Coco Vincenza's new song... and added some of his own lyrics.

"There's a lady, doing her shopping, but she dreams a big dream. It's not carrots I want, nor porridge or savoury bites... I want to be in the West End, singing under the brightest of bright lights."

Russ seemed pleased. "Great, it's writing itself."

Grace laughed.

"Do we know what charity we'll be supporting?" Mary wondered.

"Not yet," said Grace.

"I have an idea," said Russ. "Not that I want to step on anyone's toes…"

"You're not," said Grace.

"Well, there's a charity I donate to in the North that does good work with young people. It's called the Solar Music Charity, and it focuses on building confidence through learning to play an instrument and playing with others. I checked locally and there's something similar in Devon called the Carpenter-Ford Music Charity. I mean all these set-ups struggle for money."

Grace nodded. "It might be just the thing. We're not looking to run a charity. We're looking to support one."

"There's a woman called Theresa Carpenter there," said Russ. "I'll give you her details."

"Well, this is all very exciting," said Mary. "Let's have some tea, shall we?"

Without waiting for a reply, she turned on her heels and disappeared into the alcove kitchenette.

"Progress," said Grace, feeling pleased. "It's as if everything's falling into place and all the nonsense is finally behind us."

At that moment, the front door opened and an elderly woman with pink hair came in.

"Hiya!" she said, placing the door key back into her pale blue handbag.

"Um… hello?" said Grace.

"Are you the one setting up a show?"

"Yes… that's me. I'm Grace Chapman. Who might you be?"

"I'm Coco Vincenza."

Grace felt uneasy.

"You can't be. Coco's making the tea."

"Nonsense. I'm Coco Vincenza and I want to perform in your show."

"But…"

"Don't worry, I've brought a draft contract we can both sign."

The original Coco Vincenza then reappeared from the kitchenette and came to a halt.

"Ah, I see you've met my sister."

Twenty

Grace brought the car to a halt at the traffic lights. The High Street was busy with shoppers and those heading to and from the beach.

"So, Linda Colbeck is also Coco Vincenza," said Grace.

"Yes," said Russ. "Buy one, get one free. I also got the impression Linda thought there'd be money in it."

"So did I. I put her straight though."

"Is it fair to say you're now a long way out of your comfort zone?"

"Definitely. We only have two confirmed acts and they're both called Coco Vincenza."

Russ laughed but cut it short.

"Sorry."

"Don't be. It's tragically funny."

"You've miscounted though. You actually have two Cocos and one Russ Adams."

"Yes, I have you. You're all mine." It felt weird saying it. "There's also a comedian who might get back to us. Jolly Jack Ambrose. I'll tell you something though. I think the old version of me would give up."

"But not the all-new you?"

"I'm determined to help a lovely old lady… well, *two* lovely old ladies. I'm sure Linda's a good egg."

"Can I ask you something?"

"Yes?"

"Something personal?"

This was it. Whatever 'it' might be.

A car behind blared its horn.

"We have a green light," said Russ.

"Yes…" she responded, getting the car moving again. "You wanted to ask me something."

"Are you thinking of writing 'The Unforgettable' next to my name?"

She would have given him a playful shove had she not been driving.

"And why would I do that?" she demanded.

"For future generations. Just think, a hundred years from now, someone might retrieve your laptop's hard drive from a rubbish bin and wonder who this unforgettable pianist was. They could look me up in an online archive and start a fan page."

She glanced at him. His words were too over-the-top to be serious – and his crinkly smiling eyes supported her theory.

"Stop pulling my leg, Russell Adams. There's only one 'unforgettable' and that's Coco Vincenza."

"Yes, but which one?"

*

Russ was sitting at the keyboard on Grace's dining room table, playing something with an arresting slow rhythm to it.

"That's nice," said Grace. She was sitting opposite him nursing a cup of tea. "What is it?"

He looked up from the keyboard without stopping.

"Guess."

"Mozart?"

"No."

"Schubert?"

"No, it's Iron Maiden."

"Oh."

"You're not a music snob, are you?"

"I'd love to say no."

"Music is music. You can reconfigure any Heavy Metal composition for minimalist piano, just as you can play Amazing Grace as a hard rock freakout. You can speed things up or slow things down. It's all in the arrangement."

He returned to his tinkling.

"You know, there's something about Coco," he said. "To be clear, I mean Coco-Mary. I'm starstruck."

"She certainly has something."

He tinkled some more then stopped.

"I said I'd teach you a couple of pieces."

"Did you? Some other time, perhaps."

"There's no time like the present."

She thought ahead to him moving her hands and fingers into various positions on the keyboard. Then she tried to work out if that would make it more or less likely that she might do something she regretted later.

"It's a tempting offer, Russ, but I'm not tempted."

"Fair enough, but I wouldn't mind going over Coco's song with you. Perhaps you could sing her part for me."

Grace's eyes widened. "Sing?"

"I got her to sing it into my phone, remember?"

"I know but…"

"You're not shy, are you? I remember when we were young… I'm sure you sang the hits of the day."

"Yes, in the school playground when I was thirteen. We all did."

"Well, this is a hit from an earlier period. What's the difference?"

Was he teasing her? Or trying to get some kind of reaction? What if things developed. How did she feel about that possibility? Assuming she allowed that possibility to develop. In truth, she thought she might let it develop and that was a worry because she was dead against it.

"Alright. As we're friends."

He played what he presumed to be the opening chords, but there seemed to be a wall between her brain and her throat. Not just a wall, but one with added defensive fortifications.

"You missed your cue," he said.

"Sorry."

He began again.

She forced herself to sing the opening line… but it was hesitant, feeble, and devoid of passion.

He stopped playing.

"That's the trouble with getting older," he mused. "We all get out of practice with something or other."

"Sorry about that."

"That's alright."

"So… what are you out of practise with?"

He smiled. "Oh… speaking French, country dancing…"

Had they been in a ballroom, with a band, she would have danced with him there and then and whispered something French into his ear, even though she had never done either before.

"Play it again, Russ."

"Didn't Humphrey Bogart say that?"

He began playing, and this time she gave the song a little more of what she had within her. It felt too intense, and intimate, and silly to give it everything – but she knew it was an improvement.

Afterwards, he seemed happier.

"Thanks, that's really helpful. I'll get a copy of the sheet music from the publisher though. I want to get it right on the day. I certainly wouldn't want to let anyone down."

He stared at her for a moment or two. She supposed that in a Hollywood movie, he'd probably kiss her about now.

"I was thinking…" he said.

"Yes?"

"About tickets. Have you settled on prices?"

"Oh… I can't think about that at a time like this."

"A time like what?"

Make a move, you twit.

"A time like… half-four in the afternoon."

"Oh, sorry! Do you usually take a nap about now?"

"No, I do not!"

Not every day, anyway…

Grace got to her feet. She was glad he hadn't made a move. It was for the best. Relationships were too much trouble anyway. And as for a fling with a guy who walked out on her forty-four years ago…

"How about another cup of tea?" she suggested.

"Yes, good idea."

"Do you fancy anything with it?"

And again, he stared at her for a moment or two.

Twenty-One

Grace watched Russ flick through an old ledger while he polished off an oat and raisin cookie. He was sitting on her front room sofa. She was sitting opposite in an armchair.

"These are great."

"The cookie or the listings?"

"Both. But these lists are special. It's a look back into a different world."

"That's exactly what it is."

"There's a guy here… June 1963, Arnold Constant, impressions. He would have done twenty, thirty voices. I can see him now, the summer sun streaming through the window of his bed and breakfast room… him practising how to sound like the celebrities of the day. John Wayne, Rex Harrsion… A paying audience would expect the best… but now… Arnold Constant is Arnold Who? Forgotten and overlooked apart from an entry in a ledger that would have ended up in a landfill waste site had it not been rescued by your aunt."

"And here we are, bringing Arnold into our thoughts." Grace smiled. "I wonder what became of him."

"I don't think he currently has a series on Channel Four."

"No."

Russ patted the page.

"It's not a book of names, Grace. It's a book of lives captured at certain moments in time. Snapshots in writing, not in photos – more's the pity."

He turned to the end of the volume.

"1966… Billy Spottiswood, comedian." He sighed at the entry. "What became of you, Billy?"

Grace felt a pang of sympathy for the lost Billy.

"What becomes of any of us?"

"That's very philosophical. I suppose Billy and Arnold had their younger years, where they searched for those routes to the top. Then their later years, where it would all be too much bother. The great hope is that they found some happiness along the way."

"What about your younger years, Russ? You've spoken to Bev, but not to me. What became of you after you left school? Did you spend every waking hour studying music? Or did you meet anyone…?"

"A girlfriend, you mean. Yes, Ava. We were together for most of the three years."

"Wow, so…" *while I was wondering if you were thinking of me…* "…while you were working hard on your degree, you had a serious relationship?"

"Yeah, it was pretty serious around the middle year. I mean the first year was just a blast. You know, total fun."

No, I don't know.

"What about your final year?" she asked.

"Oh… less intense. Fizzled out would be a better description. We went our separate ways a couple of months before our final exams."

"Right… and after? You stayed up North?"

"I decided to do teacher training. I won't pretend I had it all worked out, I just remember another student saying they were going to do it, and it seemed like a plan. I didn't have a plan at the time, so it sort of made sense."

"And you did teacher training up there?"

"Yes, in Manchester. Part of the training included a placement at a local school. As luck would have it, they had a vacancy come up just as I qualified."

"How long did you stay there?"

"Three years. Then I fancied a change. I thought of coming home for a bit. I came down too, you know, to have a look around. But then a job came up in York and I took it. That's where I met Yvette, my wife-to-be and where I've been all this time – despite losing her to the travel bug."

Grace gave a sympathetic smile and left some space before speaking again.

"You came home though? Before York?"

"Yes."

"And you didn't say hello?"

"I did say hello – at least to Bev. I found out you were married, so I kept away. Silly, really."

"I wish you'd popped by."

"Bev told me your husband wasn't the type to welcome one of your old boyfriends."

"Bev…"

"I'm sure she meant well."

"Now she can't wait to put us together."

"Is that what you think?"

"Yes."

"I'm only here for a few weeks."

"I know."

Her feelings for him flared. How strange that her teenage love for him hadn't vanished beyond recovery.

Russ smiled. "Do you feel there's something of our past still floating around?"

"Oh, I don't know about that. We were passionate young people then."

"Yes, although…"

"Was it easy to leave Shawcross and go to Manchester?"

"Oh, well, I was eighteen and keen to leave home. I was sharing a bedroom with my brother. I had a great offer. Everything was right."

"So, it was easy enough to leave then."

"Well… not easy…"

This was it. He was going to admit he still had feelings for her. Was she ready to do likewise?

"We got on well," she said. "Or was that just me?"

"Of course it wasn't just you. I was very fond of you back then. You know I was." He peered out of the window. "I was torn for a time. I remember wishing I could study music nearby and we could stay together. At least for a bit longer. Until you grew tired of my terrible personality."

Grace laughed.

"It's a good job you went then," she teased. "I was getting really bored. Another day was probably the limit. You got out just in time."

"Well, there we are then."

He turned to face her. The seconds passed. For Grace, once again it became intense. She was sixty-two and her heart was on fire, which was probably dangerous.

Time to kiss?

But he turned away, breaking the intimacy.

"You're right," he said. "We were passionate young people then."

"And now?" she asked.

"We're two mature people."

"Exactly," she said, offering him a tried and trusted smile that always did a good job of hiding her disappointment.

Twenty-Two

"Russ and me… we're two mature people," said Grace in reply to Bev's first question no sooner she'd sat down in Bev's car.

Bev had just finished work, but she was going to drive them to Torquay to meet Theresa Carpenter of the Carpenter-Ford Music Charity.

"I know you're two mature people. I was just wondering what happened."

"We're not hot-headed youngsters, Bev."

"Yes, we've already established that. So, how did it go?"

"We talked."

"Wow, shocking. No wonder you were trying to keep quiet about it."

"If you must know, it nearly became a bit more than talk, but it fizzled out. I think I'm disappointed."

"When you say fizzled out…?"

"I think he saw the implications."

"That's good. At least I think it's good."

"Is it good? For me, I mean."

"The teenage you or the mature one?"

Grace sighed. "What a rotten situation. To want and not want… at the same time."

"I get it. It's not straightforward. You've got a limited time frame. It's all or nothing really."

"That's what it feels like. A fork in the road. Take it or leave it. Right now, we seem to be leaving it."

"I hope there aren't any self-image issues spoiling things. For what it's worth, you both look great."

"You mean great *for our age*?"

"What's the difference?"

Grace thought about that.

"You're right. It's always subjective, however young or old we are."

"Look, if I were you, I'd be going for it with abandon. We can only celebrate what we have. I mean who's to say otherwise? It's a romance, not Britain's Got Talent. There's no-one judging you. It's what's inside you… and you're a beautiful person. Admittedly it's hidden under all the crap Dennis put you through but it's there. And Russ hasn't changed. He was a good lad at school and he's a good lad now. Just older. We'll all be ashes one day, which might be tipped into a rubbish bin instead of scattered over the sea. It's not any romance, it's one with Russ, and you two are so made for each other. Also, remember this – everything you do takes up a greater percentage of the time you have left. Make a difference for the world and for Coco, yes… but make a difference for yourself too."

Bev fell silent and Grace smiled.

"Speech over?"

"Speech over."

"I do hear you, Bev. I really do."

"When was the last time?"

"The last time what?"

"Do I have to draw a picture?"

"Oh… five years or so. We were in Marbella. Dennis was drunk. And no, the earth didn't move, although the sunbed collapsed."

"What an image. I hope Theresa has some calming herbal tea."

*

Twenty minutes later, with much of the conversation being about various neutral matters, Bev followed the satnav's instruction to turn into a street of modest semi-detached houses. It wasn't long before Theresa, a cheery woman in her forties with a ponytail, was welcoming them and showing them through to a conservatory with wicker furniture overlooking a small garden.

Grace thought it was lovely. So well looked after, so cared for.

A few minutes later, sipping hot tea and nibbling on chocolate chip cookies, Theresa got down to business.

"Is there a musical connection for you?" she wondered. "Often, people who want to donate have a tie to music in some way."

"Not so much me," said Grace. "A chap who's helping me, Russ Adams, is a music teacher. He donates to the Solar Music Charity up North where he works, and we thought of looking for something similar in Devon. As I said on the phone, Bev and I had a read through the stories on your website. The work you do is wonderful."

"Thanks. You'll know then that we build confidence through learning to play an instrument. It was started by my mum and her sister: Sheila Carpenter and Maggie Ford. Mum was a music teacher; Aunt Maggie was a magistrate. They're both retired now."

Grace nodded. "You're definitely the kind of charity we should be supporting."

"Any money you can raise would help. Honestly, every penny counts."

"A lot of your success stories feature those with special needs or physical disabilities," said Bev, "but how does it work?"

"Mainly through volunteers visiting clubs and schools, but we have to pay their travel expenses and for instruments. We've also recently started funding a part-time teacher. We want to bring music to everyone and foster both individual progress and teamwork through ensemble playing – but it costs money."

Bev nodded. "Can I give you twenty pounds right now?"

"Yes, although it's best to put it through our donations page online. The higher the ongoing total there, the more confidence others have in donating."

"Alright, I'll do that."

"Thank you. The only funding we receive is through private donations. It's the lifeblood of our projects."

*

Back in the car, Grace was happy to be working on behalf of Theresa's charity. The hope now was to raise a good sum.

"Russ will be delighted," said Bev.

"He will," said Grace. "Music is close to his heart. Anyone can see that."

"He's a good man."

"I know. I was thinking…"

"Yes?"

"I was thinking I would like a relationship with the right man."

"Good for you. Might Russ be the right man?"

"That's what drains the life out of it. He won't be here long enough for me to find out."

"That's a shame. But I do get it."

The following silence felt a little heavy, so while Bev drove, Grace pulled the first volume from her bag.

"I'm so glad we found this," she said.

She flicked through slowly.

"Russ found a comedian called Billy Spottiswood. I think it was 1966. I wonder what became of him?"

"Can we look him up?" Bev wondered.

"I'm already onto it," said Grace, reaching for her phone.

An online search for comedian Billy Spottiswood didn't seem a likely source of success but the top result took her by surprise. It was a website for an actress called Lucy Brittan, whose 'About' section described the encouragement she received from her chorus line dancer mother, June Bright, and her dad, the comedian Billy Spottiswood.

Grace left a message.

Twenty-Three

On a sunny Thursday morning, Grace was on a train traversing the English countryside with a Lyric ledger open on her lap. A book of lives captured at certain moments. Snapshots in writing.

She thought briefly of Russ. Perhaps he was using her hesitation in saying anything to support his own belief – that he was too old to start a relationship. A two-and-a-half-week fling though… anyone seeing it as a compromise would have to be crazy or drunk. It really was the worst idea.

She looked down at the page.

July 1974. Rex Fogg. Comedian.

Would he still be around? She tried Facebook. Yes, he was there. Rex 'Funny Fellow' Fogg. She messaged him.

Turning the page, she found another interesting entry.

August 1974. The Bald Eagles. Comedy band.

It made her smile. No doubt a bunch of guys, perhaps thinning on top somewhat, entertaining Shawcross holidaymakers with comedy songs. She could almost hear the echo of laughter from those far-off stalls. She hoped they had an enjoyable career. She hoped they didn't split up five years later, with the drummer going back to being a plumber while the lead singer refused to give up on his dream.

Her smile fell away. She now felt melancholy. It reinforced the idea that not everyone gets a chance in life, but those that do and fail would fall into two camps: the philosophical, possibly happy ones, who can say 'at least I tried', and the tormented ones, not only lamenting what might have been, but possibly continuing to chase it without hope.

What was impossible to overlook was the notion that Time would pass anyway. And in time, the world would forget all those hopes and dreams, once so vivid and alive for the names in these pages. Maybe these names had been in the showbiz foothills on their way to the top… or perhaps they were already halfway up in the sunny uplands of the 1960s and 70s but finding the path blocked… or maybe they had been as far as they could go and were on the way down again.

She looked up and peered through the scratched glass to the fields passing outside. She enjoyed train rides where there was nothing to do. The price of the ticket gave her permission to let her mind wander freely without feeling guilty for wasting time. She wondered why she didn't do it more often.

This particular ride was taking her to Oxford, where she would meet Billy Spottiswood, the comedian from 1966. She had contacted Billy's daughter, Lucy, and it was good news. Yes, her dad was still with us, and yes he had stories from the old days. Lucy lamented that those stories would soon be lost – and this had given Grace an idea.

An hour later, she was in a cab from the station to Billy's house on the edge of Oxford. He lived in a nice little cul-de-sac with a neat front garden.

Lucy was there to greet her and show her into the back room, where a smiling Billy was seated by the open patio doors.

"Dad, this is Grace Chapman from Shawcross, who I told you about."

"Hello, hello, how are you today?" he said in a cheery tone. Grace immediately felt like an audience member.

"Hello, Billy, I'm fine, thank you. As I said to Lucy, I'm starting a collection of stories about the Shawcross Lyric Theatre in the 1960s, but any other memories you have of the business in those days would be very welcome, wherever you were at the time."

"Well, I'm eighty and I do my own gardening, but you don't want to know about that, do you."

"Your garden's lovely," said Grace, peering out at the superbly kept small patch at the back. "I've been doing my own gardening for forty years, so I can see exactly how much hard work you're putting into it."

"Ooh, I like her," Billy informed his daughter.

They soon settled down with tea and sponge slices, while Grace directed their attention to the Lyric ledger in which Billy's name first appeared.

Billy laughed. "Yes, yes, I remember. I appeared there six or seven times over as many years. If you were new and your name wasn't on the list, you'd have to wait outside the stage door until they found someone to vouch for you – even if it was raining."

Grace smiled. "A friend of mine described it as a book of lives captured at certain moments. Snapshots in writing. Now I can see it as an endless line of performers, waiting to get past my aunt, who would have been standing guard at the stage door. Do you remember Jennifer Moore?"

"I'd love to say yes, but I must have worked in a hundred theatres. Sorry."

"It's alright. The main thing now is adding to what we have with some words, photos, and video."

It didn't take long to position Billy in front of the laptop screen. The setup was enhanced by a high-definition clip-on camera and a quality microphone borrowed from Bev's husband, Jez.

"I expect you'd like me to keep it clean?" said Billy.

"That would be very helpful. Now, in your own time tell me about the Lyric. What memories do you have? Perhaps the first time you came to Shawcross…?"

"The first time…?"

"If possible."

"Right… the Shawcross Lyric. I think I first played there in 1966. I was only, what, twenty-two. It was my agent who got me the gig. He was working to get me on the variety circuit, see. I mean there were hundreds of acts who got regular work at the seaside theatres, and then more work supporting the bigger acts who got to tour with their own shows. I started to get work as a warm-up man for singers and other comedians. I mean I was working hard to make my own name, but it wasn't easy. In those days, you needed something to make you stand out. I mean everyone had a gimmick – you know, sticky up hair, parrots, oversized dungarees, puppets, all sorts. Only, I didn't have a gimmick and could never settle on one. It also helped a comedian if he could sing. I had a voice like a foghorn and couldn't hit a note. Anyway, I eventually got work at the Lyric when they had a summer season with a few big names, like Max Bygraves. Us lower ranking acts were there to fill the gaps. So, I got to spend some time there and I fell in love – with showbiz, I mean."

"So, no summer romances then?"

"Well… there was one girl. Marilyn in Leeds."

"Is she still… with us?"

He puffed out his cheeks. "No idea. I haven't been to Leeds in fifty years. I don't want to meet her either, if that's in your mind. The past is the past. I mean can you imagine meeting someone from forty, fifty years ago and going through it all again?"

"Umm… no."

"What a nightmare that would be. Unless…"

"Unless?"

"Well, unless it was that rare thing. The one that got away."

"Right. And Marilyn wasn't."

"No, she was married. And her husband found out. I got a right-hander and had to wear make-up on stage for a couple of weeks."

Lucy glared at him.

"I grew up after that. Married a fabulous lady when I was twenty-eight and we had three lovely daughters. We lost my Maggie three years ago."

Grace smiled sadly.

But what did all this mean? If she was now a collector of stories, what was the plan?

Twenty-Four

Grace was glad to be back home by five. It had been a long and tiring day, including an alarming moment when she woke up on the train coming back and momentarily thought she'd missed her stop. She hadn't but it had taken a while for her nerves to calm down.

Any thoughts of a quiet evening though were on hold. Russ had texted to ask if he might pop over. He wanted to discuss a few things.

She felt the warmth of his impending arrival but also had to consider how things might go.

What to do?

She stood and stared at herself in the mirror over the fireplace. Who was this woman staring back at her? A lady in her sixties – one who looked sensible and settled. Someone others would see as a devotee of mild murder mysteries and quiz shows on daytime television.

Few young people would understand how this woman with the greying hair could still have a heart that was open to love – and not just holding hands love, but love with passion and intensity, because she'd read a million novels full of exactly that and wanted it for herself. Why? Because it had been there once, at least the promise of it – and then more than forty years passed by while she waited for the impossible.

It occurred to her that her hair still needed doing. She would get it done.

The doorbell chimed.

She opened the door and smiled.

"Welcome," she said, wondering why she sounded like a receptionist.

"Thanks."

"A cup of tea?"

"Yes, lovely."

A moment later, with Russ in the front room, she filled the kettle in the kitchen and felt a strong urge to do something. She just wasn't sure what. She knew the choices, but she feared a mis-step might cause embarrassment.

She rinsed her Harry Potter mug and got a clean Simpsons one out for Russ. All the while, she wondered if to tell him how she felt, because she was getting fed up imagining what it would be like. She felt too vulnerable though. The conversation in her head was always going to be easier than the real thing.

But what if she could let go of her fear?

She made the tea and took the two mugs into the sitting room, where Russ looked comfortable on the sofa.

"Great," he said. "I thought we should have a catch-up."

"Yes," she said, taking the armchair opposite. "Perhaps we could start with the band. Any news?"

"Yes, there's bad news and good news."

"The bad news?"

"They split up forty years ago."

Grace slumped a little. "Well, it's not really a surprise. What's the good news?"

"One of them, Chrissie Miles, still plays – and he's in another band. He says they should be able to do it."

Grace felt a great lift in her spirits.

"That's great! When will they confirm?"

"Soon. It all sounds good though."

"Right, well…" Grace sought some inner strength. "There's something I need to tell you."

Russ frowned. "Oh?"

"It's… well… it's…"

"Billy Spottiswood?" he suggested.

"Pardon me?"

"You went to see him. I assume you want to tell me all about it?"

"Yes, I do. But…"

"But…?"

"Oh, don't pretend. You know what I mean."

"Well, your cheeks are glowing red, so either things got hot between you and Billy… or you have something else on your mind."

"Yes, I do have something else on my mind. Don't you?"

"Me? Yes, all joking aside, I feel there's still something there."

"Between us?"

"Yes, those old feelings seem to have come back. I didn't ask them to, they just reappeared. I can only imagine they must've been a lot stronger than I admitted to at the time."

Grace smiled. "Same here."

Russ shifted on the sofa and leaned forward a little.

"I told you I came back that time… when I never called on you? Bev told me you'd got married and… well… I was enormously happy for you, but also a little bit disappointed that it hadn't worked out for us. I blamed Fate."

Grace sipped her tea. The temperature in the room seemed to be getting hotter by the minute.

"It seems strange that we should get a second chance after all this time," she said.

He came over and sat on the arm of her seat.

Grace tried to relax. She wasn't a teenager. She'd been in this situation many times before. She knew the ropes. This would be it. The kiss.

He hesitated.

Does he know this is the kiss? Maybe he doesn't.

He leaned down and kissed her.

Ah, he does.

After that, things moved quickly.

*

As Friday mornings in general went, this one felt perfect. Things were amazing, life was good, and she smiled a lot. This wasn't regular behaviour for Grace Chapman.

Having texted Bev to say that Russ had stayed over, she sipped her hot coffee.

"Mmm, just what the doctor ordered."

Russ raised an eyebrow. "The coffee or…?"

She smiled. She should have felt awkward and embarrassed, but she didn't.

"Both."

He smiled too. "That's great. So, you're feeling okay. No regrets. You're saving those for later?"

"I'm fine." *No, better than fine…* "Actually, I feel pretty good."

"Life is strange," he said.

"It is."

"At the moment, it feels a little like Beethoven's Ninth."

"Does it?"

"When you come to it that first time, you sit through three long and impressive movements. Then, just as you're ready to acknowledge the completion of a satisfying symphony, there's a fourth movement that unexpectedly towers over not only the first three movements but over every symphony ever written previously."

"This is the choral piece, right?"

"Yes, Ode to Joy – where last is definitely not least."

Grace laughed. "You mean we're experiencing an Ode to Joy. Late in life, but it's unexpectedly better than what went before?"

"Oh, ignore me. I'm trying to be poetic, but I sound like a cheesy fake guru."

Grace's phone pinged.

It was a text from Bev.

'Stayed over??? How was it? Choose one of the following. Great. Terrible.'

Grace wondered what to reply. Could she say how he spent twenty minutes kissing and caressing her until, for the first time in her life, and to her utter astonishment, she found herself in the grip of an intense, joyous, breathtaking release?

She typed: 'Great!!!!!'

Bev replied.

'I demand more info!'

But Grace didn't want to get involved in a discussion.

'Let's catch up later.'

Before she could put the phone down, it pinged again.

Good grief, Bev...

But it was a text from an unknown number.

'Hello, Grace Chapman. I want to do the show. Please include me. Carol Brand, the performer known as Coco Vincenza.'

For a moment, Grace could only stare at the screen in confusion.

"This is nuts."

"What is?" Russ asked.

"There's a third Coco Vincenza."

"A *third* Coco? You're kidding me."

"I'm not. She wants to do the show."

"A third Coco. How is that possible?"

"I've no idea… but I suppose we ought to find out."

Twenty-Five

It was mid-morning and Grace was in the local corner shop getting some fresh milk and a small French baton for lunch.

Russ had gone back to his hotel room. They would meet up again later. What they might get up to was anyone's guess, although Grace reminded herself that she and Russ were both sixty-two, so it would be a mature choice.

She left the shop and set off for home floating on air. Who would have thought love could be so wonderful? She allowed herself a cheeky think back to last night. His hands, his lips, those feelings… but Mrs Frobisher, a talkative neighbour, was heading towards her.

Oh well, we can dream that bit again later.

Just then, her phone pinged. It was an email. Comedian Jolly Jack Ambrose had got back to her. He was interested in doing the show.

Twenty minutes later, Grace turned into her street, wondering how things might realistically pan out with Russ. Would she move up north to be with him? Would he consider moving south to be with her? Whichever way, there was a lightness to it, a stress-free simplicity, a refreshing vitality, and room to breathe. Perhaps marriage would follow…

She opened her front door and jolted to a standstill.

Cigarette smoke?

Her heart lurched.

No, please no.

She could hear someone moving around in the kitchen.

"That you, Grace?" the *someone* asked.

Her ex was there in her house.

"Dennis?"

He appeared at the kitchen door.

"I had a key."

"A key? I thought…"

"I brought my bags with me."

Her confusion coalesced into a thought.

"Why are you here?"

He smiled. She didn't return it. She did close the front door though; in case any passing neighbours might peer in.

"I made a mistake," he said. "I regret us breaking up. The thing is, I've left Tiff."

"But…"

"I want to try again. I think we can make a go of it."

Has he been dumped?

"You can't stay."

"Don't be unreasonable. I paid the mortgage for twenty-five years."

"But…"

"I know it's not easy for you. You're the rock in our marriage. You would never jump into bed with another man. I respect you more than you could ever know."

"This isn't right."

"It will be. In time. I'm going to take a shower. Then we'll have a nice cup of tea and a chat."

She watched him disappear upstairs. Then came the familiar sounds of someone using the bathroom. Finally, the shower was running.

Grace went into the sitting room and began pacing up and down. What should she do? She had no idea. She stopped by the patio doors and peered into the sunny garden, perhaps hoping for clarity and inspiration. A good five minutes passed without either coming to her, so she began pacing again.

The doorbell rang.

On answering it, Grace suffered another shock.

"Hi again," said a smiling Russ. He had a sports holdall with him. "It's just a few bits. Clothes, toothbrush…"

Grace was flummoxed.

"I don't… er…"

Russ's smile was unwavering.

"And I found this." He handed her a strip of photo-booth pics. "It seems my aunt ended up with a few boxes of my parents' stuff."

"Russ, I…"

"I thought it'd make more sense if I stayed with you. I mean my place at the Bay View Hotel isn't exactly five-star."

Her phone pinged. Without inviting Russ in, she checked the message. It was from Bev.

'Don't forget, you only have two weeks.'

This brought her back to her senses.

"I'm sorry, Russ… I've changed my mind."

"What? Really? It's not my thinning hair, is it?"

"No…" Tears sprang to her eyes. In that moment, she was certain that she loved him. But she wouldn't risk everything for a man who would be gone in a couple of weeks.

She wanted to close the door. But she could only bite her lip and stare into his eyes. She wanted him but she was in her sixties, not her twenties. Stability. That was the key to having a settled future.

Russ looked crestfallen.

"Grace? What's happened?"

Then there were feet on the stairs, coming down.

"Hello?" said Dennis to the visitor on the doormat.

"Oh," said Russ. "Who are you?"

Dennis seemed most put out.

"Who am I? I'm the homeowner. Who are you?"

Grace wanted to vanish into thin air. Her innards were churning. She felt sick.

"I'm er… are you Grace's husband?"

"Yes. Grace, what's going on?"

"This is Russ – an old friend from school."

But Russ could only focus on Dennis.

"You're back?"

"Yes, I'm back. What's it got to do with you?"

Russ shook his head.

"Why have you come back? You're all wrong for Grace. You stifle her. You make her invisible."

"How dare you. Clear off before I call the police."

"I'm sorry, Russ," said Grace.

With a regret that made the door weigh a hundred tons, she pushed it to.

"What is he – a nutcase?" Dennis fumed.

"It's alright. He's gone now." But all she could think was – *now what?*

Dennis huffed and went into the kitchen, the matter seemingly closed. A moment later, the kettle was being filled. Coffee and biscuits would follow.

Grace looked at the strip of photos in her hand. Then she looked in the hall mirror again. Her hair still needed doing.

It could wait.

The most important thing now was to let Bev know.

Twenty-Six

The following Monday, Grace met the three Coco Vincenzas at Mary's place. Feeling a little closed down by her renewed matrimonial commitments, she had agreed over the phone to taking them out to the pub. She was regretting it now as she beheld the trio.

"I'm sorry I'm late," she said. "The cab was delayed in getting to me."

"It's Carol who should apologise for being late," said Coco-Mary.

Silver-haired Carol curtsied theatrically.

"So, three sisters…" Grace mused.

"I promise you that's it," said Linda.

"Yes, well…" *Three's enough.*

There was something about them though…

"Now what's all this about a cab?" said Mary. "Where's the car?"

"My husband needed it to pop into town."

She and Mary exchanged a glance, but nothing was said.

"Let's go," said Carol. "You can tell me all about the show on the way."

"There's not much to tell," said Grace.

"Fair enough – as long as I, Coco Vincenza, get to sing."

Coco-Mary and Coco-Linda both scoffed.

"Let's get going," Grace suggested prior to turning for the door. "We'll find somewhere nearby."

"No, let's go down to the seafront," said Carol.

"How about the Red Lion?" said Linda.

"That's not near the sea."

"No, it's on the green side of town and it has a lovely beer garden." She turned to Grace. "You don't get many tourists there either."

"Okay," said Grace, "I'd better phone for a cab."

"No, we'll get the bus," Carol insisted.

Grace sighed.

"Okay."

Five minutes later, the four of them were standing at the bus stop, where Grace found herself trying to take a step or two away from the sisters to assure passers-by that these three were on their own. But Carol and Linda somehow got either side of her and linked their arms with hers. All was lost.

Still, it didn't matter. An hour in the pub would serve as a farewell event. After that, she would turn away from the three Cocos, forget the charity show, and go back to her old life. She was already wondering why she'd got herself into such a pickle. It was just as well Dennis knew nothing about it.

"We're sisters," said Linda, somewhat unnecessarily. "When the nostalgia thing started in the 80s, I picked up the name and carried it on. At first, I mentioned I wasn't the original Coco, but people didn't listen or care, so I stopped saying so."

"That's when I saw an opportunity," said Carol. "At the time, the Pet Shop Boys had teamed up with Dusty Springfield, so I teamed up with a synth duo called The Shot-Put Boys."

"Then Mary made a comeback," said Linda.

"Three Cocos…?" Grace could just about imagine it.

"Yes, three Cocos," said Mary. "How do you think we managed to perform in England, Ireland and Germany at the same time?"

Linda laughed. "It was me who gate-crashed a pop awards party and got my face in the papers – partially blocked by Gary Barlow."

"You can photoshop faces out nowadays," said Carol.

"Ooh, good idea – remove Gary Barlow's face."

"No, I meant remove yours."

Fortunately, any chance of it descending into a squabble was cut short by the arrival of the bus.

As they boarded, the three Cocos hurried straight to the vacant rear seats – Grace guessed it dated back to childhood.

She smiled at the half dozen passengers as she followed the sisters, but she chose to sit in the row in front of them.

"You're married, are you?" Linda asked from behind.

"Yes… I've been married for forty years." She imagined that Mary might be staring in surprise, but those piercing eyes would only have the back of Grace's head to glare at.

"That's staying power," said Carol. "You deserve a medal."

Grace felt dispirited. A medal. But this was the state of her life. She just had to put on a cheery face and get on with it. She wouldn't let them dictate the conversation though.

"I really don't see why we're on a bus," she said turning to face them. "A cab would have been better."

"We love the bus," said Linda. "It reminds us of the good old days."

"Ah, the good old days," said Carol. "We grew up in Bournemouth until we were nine…"

"Eleven," said Linda.

"Thirteen," said Mary. "Then we moved to Torbay."

"What was so special about the bus?" Grace wondered.

"What was so special?" Mary sounded surprised. "Okay, imagine the scene… back of the bus… three girls… a captive audience…"

"Ah, I get it," said Grace, the concept dawning on her. "You sang."

"We *performed*, Grace. We *performed*."

"Twice daily," said Carol, proudly. "Once on the way to school, once on the way back."

"To a packed house… or bus," said Linda.

"To and from school," said Grace. "I can picture it. It must have been quite a thing."

"It's no good just picturing it," said Mary, which gave Grace a terrible sense of premonition.

"It'll be our stop in a few minutes," she said.

"Plenty of time," said Carol. "Girls?"

Grace smiled at the other passengers apologetically and wondered if to get off at the next stop. But from behind her came something extraordinary.

Instant harmonies. Three parts. As if they'd been practicing.

She knew the song, too. 'Mr. Sandman'. Their voices had a slight fragility to them, from age, of course, but they were in tune to a professional degree with not a fraction of a second to separate them in their timing. She had pretended to not be with them, but the feeling now…? It was nuts, it was insane, but for some reason she was proud of them.

And then they finished beautifully, with a flourish. Immediately, the half dozen passengers burst into applause.

"Wow," was all Grace could say. They really did have something. But she was about to walk away, wasn't she?

Just then, her phone pinged. It was Russ.

'If you're still going ahead, the band are happy to appear for free. Let me know.'

Twenty-Seven

Grace was standing at the bar of the White Swan, a lovely old pub on the edge of town. The three Cocos were outside, having grabbed a table with a bright yellow parasol in the sunny beer garden.

While waiting to be served, Grace decided something. Not only would she put the show on, she would also start 'enjoying' the task. It was pointless hating the difficulties. It was a matter of embracing every aspect of it. Wholeheart-focus or something. This is what Carol had burbled on about during the two-minute walk from the bus stop.

To Grace, it was what some people called hokum, but why not hum a happy tune while getting on with it. It wasn't so silly. Dennis would understand. He wouldn't call her silly. He might offer to help her.

Although…

She recalled her attempt to paint the garden shed. She'd bought the right wood preserve and brush. She enjoyed applying it too – for twenty minutes until Dennis came out to observe, and give tips, and take the brush to demonstrate, and then carry on with it himself while she made a cup of tea. That evening, the shed looked lovely, and Dennis ate his dinner while complaining how he always had to do everything himself.

As for the show – still in her own hands for now – she possibly had a comedian, and she definitely had three singing sisters, a pianist, and a band.

"What can I get you?" asked the young chap behind the bar.

"Right, four small lager shandies and four cheese salad sandwiches, please. We're outside, table number six."

"I'll do the drinks now. Sandwiches – five minutes. I'll bring them out."

She soon had the four drinks on a tray and was at the door to the garden, which a young woman was holding open for her.

"Thanks," she said.

Stepping over the threshold, she could see the sisters farther up the busy beer garden, where Mary was laughing about something.

Grace halted. She had seen that look before. It was in a photo taken at Bev's sixtieth birthday bash. The person in the photo was Grace herself. She knew it, of course. She had guessed a while back. Mary Smith, a seventeen-year-old singer and her best friend Jen, whose elder sister, Olive couldn't have children…

She turned and re-entered the pub, placing the tray of drinks on the nearest free table. She took a seat. She felt weak.

A young man stopped by her.

"Are you alright? You look pale."

"As if I've seen a ghost, you mean?"

"I was going to say *huge tax bill*, but yes."

"I'm fine. I skipped breakfast. Bad mistake."

Mary Smith was her mum. Gordon had to be her married name.

She took a steadying breath, rose to her feet, and took the tray of drinks into the garden. Despite the general hubbub, she could hear Linda.

"You can't drop out."

"I didn't say I'd drop out," Mary insisted. "I said I wouldn't perform solo. My voice isn't at its best. It must be the dry air or something. Singing with you and Carol is fine. We'll do a couple of numbers together. Three, maybe."

"What about your hit? It doesn't have any harmonies."

"We'll adapt it."

Grace was hearing the words but was having trouble processing them.

"Here she comes!" cheered Carol.

"The sandwiches won't be long," said Grace, placing the tray in the middle of the table. She then took a seat with them and tried to smile at the antics of a family that had rejected her.

Her thoughts turned dark. Being given away as a baby might not have produced instant emotional damage and lifelong harm, but suddenly everything was raw – as if it had just happened.

Then something struck her. It was almost comical. She had ruled out doing anything as tough as running a marathon to make a difference. But this? How was working with a secret mother easier?

She took a sip of shandy. This was all about raising money for a worthwhile cause. Despite what she now knew, she would work with Mary and her sisters for the next couple of weeks. After that, she would move on.

Mary, her mother, smiled at her.

"So, Grace, how are we doing?"

"We're short of performers. I've got a possible comedian – Jolly Jack Ambrose. Do you know him?"

All three shook their heads.

"Well, he's yet to confirm, and I've not seen him perform. We'll see. There's another comedian I'm hoping to hear from. Rex 'Funny Fellow' Fogg. I've no idea if he'll be interested. I'm also going to contact the local comedy club. It might be worth having a couple of younger comedians to keep up the energy levels. I'm hoping we might be able to attract a Master of Ceremonies too. We need someone who knows how to pull everything together in front of an audience."

"It's going well then," said Mary.

"Yes, I'm hoping we can all walk away from this with our heads held high."

Twenty-Eight

A couple of days later, Grace was at home, half-listening to the radio while giving the kitchen worktops a quick squirt and wipe. Dennis, who was working from home, had popped out to get a newspaper, which usually meant he wanted to make a private phone call. She could track the progress of his affairs from this alone.

Her phone rang. It was Russ.

"Hello," she said as she paced into the hall bound for the sitting room.

"Hey, is it okay to talk?"

She thought of Dennis talking and walking outside, and realized she was doing the same indoors.

"Yes, of course."

"I was just wondering about the show."

"Yes, it's on."

"Oh right. I wasn't sure. Thanks for clearing that up. Are you sure you're okay?"

"I'm fine." Grace had no intention of feeling anything. All senses would remain shut down for the duration. Being back with her husband would work. She would make it work.

"Grace," he said, "I only wanted to make you happy. I'm sorry it didn't work out."

Her heart jumped a little at him saying her name. Okay, so she did feel something for him. But why? It served no useful purpose. If it wasn't for the show…

"How much are we hoping to raise?" he asked.

And that was the whole point. This was about raising funds.

"A few thousand, perhaps?"

It suddenly occurred to her that she could cancel the show and transfer that amount to the charity from her savings account, which was about to be boosted by a couple of thousand inherited from dear Aunt Jen's solicitor. In fact, wasn't that the best idea of all?

"Will you add anything?" he asked. "Only, I was thinking of adding a little myself."

"Yes… actually, it might be best if I put a couple of thousand in and cancel the show. It would save a lot of trouble."

"A simple donation, you mean. Yes, I can see that working. Will you tell the three Cocos, or shall I?"

Grace sighed. She was looking for a shortcut to avoid further pain. But putting on a show, having wonderful performers, and gathering a big audience would make it a landmark event. It would be enjoyed and talked about. The charity would be mentioned in lots of circles, including in the local press. Others might want to look into its work and contribute – not just money, but time. Who could know the greater benefits a show would bring about?

"If we go ahead, we'll need more performers. And we'd need tickets to go sale by the weekend."

"That's more like it."

"Russ… let me get back to you tomorrow."

She ended the call and went straight to the Lyric ledgers. Sitting at the dining table, she stared at the names on the page. Was this really going to work? Seeing it to its conclusion was one thing – but what if the whole thing turned into a gigantic failure?

She grabbed her phone and made a call.

"Bev?"

"Hi, how's going?" a cheery voice came back at her.

"I'm thinking of asking another pianist to take over."

"Really?" Bev sounded shocked. "You mean cheat on Russ?"

"Don't be ridiculous. It's not the same thing at all."

"Yes, it is. It's exactly the same."

Grace got up and went into the kitchen.

"Bev, it's turned into Lord of the Rings."

"No, it hasn't."

"It has. It's like Frodo and the ring."

"How?"

"Frodo gets the ring and has a simple task. To take it to some friendly elves in a lovely forest where everyone sings and eats salad. Easy-peasy. Only, when he gets there, they say, actually the ring needs to go much farther… to Mount Doom, and we've chosen *you* to take it there."

"Grace… helping three Coco Vincenzas is not the same."

"It absolutely is."

The sound of a key in the front door lock was followed the door opening.

"I'll call you back, Bev."

She ended the call and then filled the kettle.

"Grace, I want to get it right," said Dennis at the kitchen doorway. "We'll repair our marriage. What can be more important than that?"

She put the kettle on the side but didn't switch it on.

"I strayed," she said.

"What?"

She turned to face him.

"I strayed."

"With another man?"

"Yes."

Dennis heaved a great big sigh. He looked genuinely surprised.

"Well, we're a fine pair! Both of us being disloyal and dishonest. I think we owe each other some extra effort, don't you?"

She said nothing, so he continued.

"If you can forgive my lapses, I'll forgive yours. I'll be honest, I never thought of you as someone who would jump into bed with another man, but it's fine. I forgive you. We'll make a fresh start."

She swallowed her pride.

"I'm sorry it happened."

He nodded. "Well, it looks like we have a lot of work to do."

"Yes, we do."

She turned and switched the kettle on. They would try again because she had never shied away from her responsibilities. She and her husband were on different pages, but that wasn't important.

Suddenly, he was at her side. He leaned forward… and switched the kettle off.

"Coffee can wait. Let's go upstairs."

Her heart sank a little, but she followed him. Being loyal meant no half-measures.

A few minutes later, they were on the bed and about to make love for first time in years. There were no preliminaries.

She refused to think of Russ, despite his kindness and attention having left an emotional mark. His focus on her had been wonderful, but wrong. Theirs was never some silly, innocent, belated coming-of-age romance. It had been two adults getting up to adult things, even though he'd made her feel special.

Dennis blew his nose and got alongside her. On the plus side, it would all be over quickly. But that wasn't important.

"Ready?" he asked.

A question… which needed an answer.

She thought about it. Was she ready?

"No," she replied.

He frowned at her.

"What's wrong?"

"I can't."

"I thought you wanted to."

"Sorry."

She got off the bed and pulled her dressing gown on.

"Oh well," he said, eyeing her. "Maybe tomorrow."

"Dennis, I expect to be treated more sensitively when we're… you know."

He sat up and shook his head.

"Have you been reading those magazines again? We're just a normal couple, okay? This is our marriage. It's how things are. We have to work together to make it a success."

"I know, but we need to be a team."

"I'm going out later," he said. "A business colleague."

She nodded. It was through his work that he'd met the other women. They seemed to be attracted to him.

Whether that was his personal magnetism or his seniority in the company, she had no idea.

While he dressed, she went downstairs in her dressing gown to make a hot drink. Dennis would retire from work in a couple of years. Then they'd get to spend all day every day together. If she could hang on, they'd be fine. All it needed was for her to understand that they were a normal couple and that this was all anyone in their sixties could reasonably expect from life.

Twenty-Nine

The following morning, Grace was at the seafront mulling things over. While life with Dennis had now been fixed, the situation with Mary Gordon was still up in the air. The question was – should she confront her with what she knew? In truth, it seemed too complicated.

She sighed and switched her thoughts to the concert and the charity… and to making a difference. Certainly, the marathon seemed a better option than ever. Perhaps she could run the first mile, walk the second, and crawl the rest of the way. It would be a lot less painful than her current stupid path.

In fact, Fate had done such a bad job of finding the *right* path, it occurred to her to simply start walking to see where her feet would take her.

Fate, Feet… was there a difference?

She set off – and her feet headed towards Coco's place.

Oh well, I may as well follow them there.

Her feet then decided to divert to the bus stop.

Half an hour later, she was welcomed by Mary.

"Tea? Coffee? I've got some chocolate hobnobs."

"Tea, please."

Mary reappeared holding the pack of biscuits.

"Are you putting this show on or not?"

"Yes, it's just that…"

"It's a yes or it's a no. Any doubts means no."

"It's not easy. My husband is back, and I've got commitments."

Mary put the biscuits on the table.

"If I can give you one tip?"

"Yes?"

"If you find someone is draining you of energy, walk away."

"Did you read that in a book?"

"No, it was one of the Sunday newspapers a while back."

"Well, I'll think about it."

"Trust me, you'll save yourself a lot of pain."

Grace decided it was time.

"Speaking of pain, I know who you are."

Mary considered it for a moment.

"Same here."

"And yet no reaction when I showed up here that first time?"

"I cried. You saw me."

"Ah, the tears for Aunt Jen."

"Most of them were for you."

"I don't want them."

Coco shrugged. "I'd love to put things right. I just don't know how."

"I asked why you changed your name to Coco Vincenza. You suggested Mary Gordon wasn't a showbiz name. But you wouldn't have been Gordon then."

"No, I told a big fib. I wasn't against you finding out…"

"You wanted me to work for it?"

"It's not that. You've had an entire life without me. I thought it might be best if you walked away without joining up the dots."

"What about Mary Gordon? Another fake name?"

"No, no, definitely not. I was Mary Smith until I married a fine man called Jimmy Gordon. That was in London in 1968. I stayed there for forty years. Do you know Camden Town?"

"I've heard of it."

"Well, that's where we were. Then Jimmy died and I came back to Devon. I mean you and I weren't likely to recognize each other, which seemed to be for the best."

Grace nodded a little.

"So, you were in Coronation Way in Polcombe for a while."

"For fifteen years, yes. I've not been at Woodbury Lodge long."

Grace was pleased to finally have some truth.

"What about Aunt Jen? I'm assuming she knew all this."

"Yes, she did. She was my best friend. If you're ever lucky enough to have a best friend, hold onto them. They're a gift. They keep us sane."

"Why didn't she tell me?"

"Because her big sister, Olive, who you rightly called Mum, didn't want you to know about a good-time girl called Mary Smith."

Grace could easily believe it. "Mum was very moral. She was a good woman."

"She was indeed. A very good woman who couldn't have children. I was her little sister's best friend who got into trouble."

The whole picture was now falling into place.

"Was Aunt Jen some sort of go-between?"

"Yes, she was someone you could always rely on to get things done."

"And… was I an unwanted package?"

"Oh, please don't say that!" Mary's eyes filled. "I wanted you with all my heart!"

A moment of silence passed before she spoke again.

"Things were very different in the early 1960s. We were a million miles from the peace and love of the late-60s. When you were born, it was still a post-War period with Victorian values. The world was in black and white. It didn't turn into colour until around 1967. I blame the Beatles."

Grace smiled a little.

"Did you have more children?"

"Two more, both stillborn. It left me empty."

Another silence ensued.

"What about me?" Grace eventually asked. "How did I come about?"

"Oh… I fell into a man's arms, a man I loved. I thought he was going to ask me to marry him, so I gave myself to him. It was wonderful for a few months and then he left, and I fell apart."

Grace had come to Mary half-wanting to get angry. But something about the moment of giving she'd described… the same moment Grace had experienced with Russ, only for him to leave beforehand. How were she and Mary different?

She found an unexpected tear rolling down her own cheek.

"Who's that for?" Mary asked.

"All of us," said Grace.

Mary smiled sadly. "Ah well… what's done is done. At the end of it all, we're only human."

Grace nodded. "If you're okay with it, I'd like us to be friends."

Mary's smile broadened.

"I think that's a very good idea."

For the first time in over sixty years, mother and daughter embraced. It was deeply felt and lasted some time before they pulled apart.

"I'm sure I was meant to be making us some tea," said Mary.

Grace followed her to the kitchenette and watched while Mary filled the kettle and plugged it in.

"Tell me, do your sisters know who I am?"

"No, not at all," Mary replied. "All those years ago, I never told them your name. They'll never know unless you decide it's time."

"Let's leave it then. At least for now. I don't think I have the capacity."

"You'll always be in charge of that decision."

Just then Grace's phone pinged.

It was a text from Russ.

'Can we talk?'

"Sorry, Mary. I have to call Russ."

"You do that, and I'll have a nice cup of tea waiting for you."

Grace smiled and headed to the sofa, from where she made the call.

"Hi," she said. "Is everything alright?"

"Um, Grace… I'm heading back home a bit earlier than planned."

A sense of alarm gripped her.

"Why? What's happened?"

"Coming back hasn't worked."

"Oh Russ…"

"It was brilliant to see you again. You're still as lovely as ever. Now, as for the show, you've got the band, so you'll be fine. I'll text you my mate's contact number so you can stay on top of it."

"Right… I…" But she had no idea what else to say.

"Bye, Grace."

"Bye."

She ended the call and let out a long sigh.

Where was she in life?

Nowhere.

Worse than nowhere.

No, that was wrong. She was very much somewhere. She had stability. Marriage to Dennis was what she'd signed up for. These emotions were only drawing her away from that stability. She needed to switch them off again.

Mary appeared with their tea.

"Here we are."

"Mary, I can't put the show together."

"Are you sure." Mary put their drinks on the table. "You still have a week and a bit."

"It's beyond me. I just can't do it. Sorry."

"Is Russ the problem?"

"No, this is down to me. I started out with the best intentions, but… I'll donate some money. The charity won't lose out."

Mary sighed. "Ah well, it was a nice idea, but I'm probably a little too old anyway."

Grace felt bad, but it was over. Making a difference had come to nothing and The Unforgettable Coco Vincenza would remain as Fate had intended all along – completely and utterly forgotten.

Thirty

It was just after five p.m. on Friday. The breeze off the sea blew through Grace's hair and those waves kept on rolling in. In every way, she felt small and insignificant – which was the best way to repel any feelings of disappointment. After all, how could anyone be disappointed when they didn't amount to much in the first place.

No, the past was gone. It was done. The here and now was all that mattered. And, in the here and now, hadn't she made some grown-up decisions?

Yes, the situations with both Russ and Mary had been settled and she had welcomed back her husband. If nothing else, she was a capable woman.

Some people struggled with big events, but not her. It was like clearing out Aunt Jen's flat. Daunting at first, but you just have to roll those sleeves up and get on with it.

Go Grace Chapman!

All that remained was to ignore the disguised doorways to the past. These were the random things that could trigger a memory.

Random things such as a cat or a piano.

She thought of a cat… and how Aunt Jen must have felt taking the daughter to the real mother's home. But it had been a mercy mission. And what would a five-year-old Grace have made of it anyway? They were just feeding a cat. No harm done. And now, a cat might trigger the entire episode, but it had an ending as such.

As for a piano? That might be a different matter.

Bev came to halt beside her.

"It was fun while it lasted then?"

"Beverley Sullivan… how about I buy you a drink."

"Sounds like a plan."

"Now that it's all in the past I can wear the T-shirt: 'Been there, done that.' Moving on – that's the main thing now."

"Yeah, about the 'been there, done that' T-shirt. You didn't put on a charity concert. And as for Russ, you didn't get the guy."

"I'm not the right person to put on a concert and I never wanted the guy in the first place. Actually, why are you here?"

"Your text said, *I'm at the seafront – Help!* For some reason, I took it as an invitation. You also said you're cancelling the show, and you won't be seeing Russ again."

"It wasn't meant to be. That's what people say, isn't it."

"What people?"

"People who cancel charity concerts and ditch the man they… like."

"Oh, *those* people. Yes, that's exactly what they say… when they want to convince themselves they haven't made a gigantic mistake."

"Did you know Mary Gordon's my mum?"

"Um… yes, I did."

Grace was stunned.

"Bev, you're meant to say no."

"Look, this is all a bit awkward. First things first, in fifty years, you never once told me your real mum's name was Mary, and neither did your aunt, so don't go thinking that. The way I knew of her was by a black and white photo…"

"Lizzie?"

Bev's eyebrows lifted a little.

"Your Aunt Jen told me a singer called Coco Vincenza was your mum, and that Coco and Lizzie were the same person."

Grace puffed out her cheeks.

"All these years and you never told me."

"No, hang on, Jen only told me a couple of weeks before she died."

Graced was double-stunned. "What?"

"She said she'd left it too late and apologized for passing the buck to me."

"And you never told me?"

"I thought the opportunity for you to meet Coco might be enough."

"I can't believe it."

"I know, I'm sorry."

"I don't understand though. I found Coco through a complete coincidence."

"No, you didn't."

"Yes, I did. We found those books and then I found her name in the first volume."

"Fair enough."

"No… hang on…"

Grace felt as if she'd stepped off a cliff edge.

It took a moment to recover.

"Bev… you led me to those books and to Coco's entry."

Bev sighed. "I was helping your aunt… you know, with her final wishes. I should've been thinking more about you though."

Grace was having trouble seeing which way to turn.

"I honestly don't know what to say."

"It was Jen's last day at home. She went into hospital the following morning. You were there all the time from then on, giving her the familiar comforting presence she needed."

Grace tried to find some forgiveness. There was still something bothering her though.

"Did you go to see Coco?"

"No, never. I just pointed you in the right direction, that's all."

"Aunt Jen, the puppet-master. All those years ago, she wrote 'the unforgettable' in front of Coco's name and then… right at the very end… she showed it to you and got you to steer me towards her."

She looked to Bev for a nod or a shrug – but Bev's expression was one of mild alarm.

And then it hit home.

"Oh, Bev… no…"

"Sorry, Grace."

"She didn't, did she?"

Bev nodded. "She wrote 'the unforgettable' in front of Coco's name a few weeks ago."

Grace blinked away a tear.

There was too much to take in.

She had seen everything, and she had seen nothing.

"My real mum…?" she eventually said.

Bev nodded, perhaps with hope. "Yes?"

"What did Aunt Jen tell you about her?"

"Oh… she told me your adoptive mum, Olive, didn't like your real mum."

"Chalk and cheese, you mean. Or sensible versus reckless?"

"Well, your real mum got pregnant at seventeen. Olive feared you might share her traits, so she told Jen to keep the story a secret. It wasn't a casual request. She made Jen swear to it."

"Aunt Jen certainly kept her word."

"Yes, but she felt you deserved to know. That's why she told me. She knew we'd been best friends for fifty years so… she knew I'd help you discover the truth for yourself. Only, I made complete mess of it."

Now it was Bev's turn to blink away a tear.

Grace walked on. Bev followed.

"Grace, I got it wrong. I wish I knew how to make it up to you."

"You got Russ wrong too. I wish you'd never set us up."

"I'm so sorry about Russ too. Your aunt thought—"

"My aunt??"

Grace came to a halt again.

Bev stopped beside her. "She pulled those strings too."

Grace was gobsmacked.

"How!"

"She remembered Russ from all those years ago. She remembered how much she liked him and how he made you shine – her words, not mine. All I did was tell Jen he was coming to Shawcross for a few weeks, and she leapt on it. She said your Dennis was the most self-centred, stifling, inconsiderate man she'd ever clapped eyes on. I could've argued, but Dennis had fled the roost and you and Russ made sense to me too."

For several seconds, Grace beheld her friend… and then sighed.

"We've known each other too many years to fall out."

Bev smiled bravely.

"What, even if I've completely ruined your life?"

Grace smiled too, but warmly. "I think there's a law… something about if you've been friends for half a century, you're not allowed to fall out."

"Oh right. Yes, I've heard of that law too."

"Anyway, I've made friends with Mary now. That's something worthwhile."

"I'm glad."

"So, we move on. Onward and upward. Or at least onward to the pub."

They resumed their walk with Grace linking her arm through Bev's.

"You know what, Bev – as for *him*… it was like being on a journey and finding the right road, only to realize it wasn't the right road after all. That happened to me once when I drove to Appledore."

Bev frowned. "Sorry, but which *him* are we talking about?"

"Isn't it obvious?"

"It's not what I'd call crystal clear."

"I'm talking about… *him*… Russ… obviously."

"Ah, that *him*. All's well that ends well then. You had a narrow escape with Russ but now you're free to be with Dennis again."

"It's for the best."

"Hey, you got to choose the life you wanted."

"Exactly. How many people get to make that kind of choice?"

"You're right again. How many people get to spend the rest of their life with Dennis."

"Exactly, Bev. I couldn't have said it any clearer myself."

As they approached the Golden Lion pub, Grace thought back to the three Cocos singing on the bus… and to an idiot crashing his shopping trolley into hers. But that was all in the past now. The Cocos were returning to life as Mary, Linda and Carol… and Russ would by now be on a northbound train, never to return.

Thirty-One

It was half-nine on Saturday morning. Grace had been up since seven. Finally, she could hear him moving around upstairs. He was speaking to someone on the phone. No doubt, he'd soon come downstairs looking casual. While he wore a smart suit and tie for professional reasons, he liked polo shirts and elasticated waistband chinos at home.

The routine of it was okay, Grace supposed. They would muddle through the day doing whatever best pleased him. Then later, they would have dinner and watch a bit of TV. Dennis liked those 'house in the country' shows where he could shout at the screen how rubbish the house was, or how they should knock that wall through and extend out the back. Grace would say the people were working within a budget, but he'd say they could get a bigger mortgage like other people have to. He would then spend time explaining to her how hard he'd had to work to pay off their mortgage and how he shouldn't have to explain himself, even though in the whole time they'd been married she never once knew the size of their mortgage or the monthly repayments because he dealt with all their finances.

No, it was fine. Maybe later they wouldn't go straight to sleep. She'd happily accept that. It was all part of married life.

He finally came down and shared an insight.

"Never trust an Accounts Manager under the age of forty."

It was in that moment, as she struggled to digest his advice, that she realised there was just one thing she wanted to say to him.

"Dennis?"

"Yes?"

"I'd like you to leave."

He looked shocked.

That didn't surprise her. She was shocked herself.

"What did you say?" he demanded.

"I'd like you to leave this house and never come back."

"Why?"

"Because I can't go on like this. Please get your things together and go."

"You can't be serious."

"I am."

He stared at her with a growing anger, but then huffed and stormed off into the sitting room.

She soon heard him on the phone. He was talking to the other woman. He was trying to talk her round. He stepped out onto the patio, so she went upstairs and listened at the back bedroom window. Whatever he'd said, he was getting nowhere. Tiff didn't want him.

She hurried downstairs again and went into the kitchen. He saw her through the window, but she was simply filling the kettle.

He came back in, leaving her to wonder what he'd do next. Would he try to sweet talk her into submission too?

"I'm going ahead with the divorce," he announced, which came as a reasonable development.

"Okay," she said.

"Tiff wants me back. She realised she couldn't be apart from me."

Grace stared at him. *You liar.* She said nothing though.

He looked as if he might say something more but changed his mind and headed back to the stairs.

"Did you ever love me?" she asked, following him.

He stopped on the first step and turned, now towering over her.

"What kind of question is that?"

"Are you able to answer it?"

He shrugged. "I did once, sort of. But let's be honest with each other, we lost it years ago. I sometimes wonder if we ever truly had it in the first place."

Grace shuffled from one foot to the other.

"I gave everything to our marriage, Dennis."

"No, you didn't."

"What?" This was a new shock altogether.

"You held back a lot of yourself."

Grace was furious.

"I… I wanted children. You didn't. We went along with your wishes because I thought it was more important to honour our marriage."

"It doesn't matter now. You're free to do whatever you like. Once the divorce is finalised I might marry Tiff, or I might break free and start again somewhere else. Either way, you can stay here until you sell the place. We'll split the money fifty-fifty. You should be able to get a nice little flat with that."

She wanted to cry over forty wasted years with a man who had only 'sort of' loved her, and only at the beginning of their time together. She wanted to fall on the floor and roll around blubbing. She had completely messed up her life. But she wouldn't do any of that. Not in front of him.

She puffed out her cheeks.

"Well, no more pain and frustration then," she said.

"No."

He was about to turn to climb the stairs, but she had something more on her mind.

"Dennis? Can I just say something?"

He paused on the half-turn.

"Yes?"

She wanted to say so much. She even had some juicy words at the ready. But no. There was another way.

"Best of luck," she said.

It was clear that he almost smiled – *almost*, but not quite. Instead, he gave the faintest of nods.

She waited for him to get his things. It only took five minutes – mainly because it was just some clothes and essential paperwork.

"Right then," he said. "I don't want anything here. You can sell it or give it away."

"What about your DVDs…?"

"Give them to your charity shop."

"Right." He didn't know that Heart Sense had closed down. There didn't seem much point in telling him.

She watched him put his bags in their midnight blue Polo. It seemed strange to be observing something so profound that would appear so routine to anyone else.

A neighbour across the street nodded.

Grace nodded back.

For all the world, Dennis was simply off on one of his business trips to London or the Midlands.

He got in the car without looking back.

A moment later, he pulled away and turned the corner into the lane that led to the main road. She watched closely until a bush and a wall blocked any further tracking of his progress. Dennis had gone, never to return.

It was a huge moment, and yet seemingly no moment at all. The rest of the world wouldn't have noticed. The rest of the *street* hadn't noticed. In the end, it was just a man driving off somewhere.

Back inside the house, it seemed awfully quiet.

She went upstairs and sat on the bed. A moment of peace. She got up again and went to the top drawer in the tall chest of drawers. Rifling through the junk of old phones, watches, sunglasses, pens, chargers, travel tissues, and many other items, she retrieved a strip of four photos she'd buried there. Just like Mary and her man, these two – herself and Russ – were making faces at the camera.

She thought about what Mary had said. "Early sixties, taken in London. He was a funny guy, but he went back to America."

Perhaps in years to come someone would ask her about her photos. Perhaps she would say, "Mid-seventies, taken in Devon. He was a funny guy, but he moved up North."

She studied the strip. Four teenage moments. The photo at the top suggested uncertainty.

The photo below it suggested Russ had said or done something silly, because she was laughing.

The third photo suggested this nonsense had continued, because they were both laughing their heads off.

The last photo, at the bottom of the strip, said something else. While he laughed, she was glancing sideways at him as if, even then, she knew this was the man for her.

And now he was gone.

She tore the strip in half and threw it in the waste basket.

With a sigh, she left the bedroom and went downstairs. There, she sat in the back room overlooking the garden.

She thought of putting the radio on and listening to a talk show but stopped short of pressing the button. This was still her moment, however low she felt. She couldn't share it with voices coming at her one-way across the airwaves.

That didn't mean she couldn't share it at all though.

She texted Bev with the latest news.

After all, wasn't that what best friends were for?

Thirty-Two

ONE YEAR LATER

The thing with late August in Shawcross was the unpredictability of the weather. The previous week had been one of wind and rain coming in south-west from a stormy Atlantic. But now, thanks to the weather coming up from hot, dry Africa and Spain in the south, the temperature had ramped up and the sun was shining from a clear blue sky.

The town itself was alive with the happy buzz of tourists enjoying their time at the seaside. Grace was standing by the sea wall watching plenty of them on the beach either sunning themselves or playing in the breakers.

She thought of the text she'd received a few minutes ago from Billy Spottiswood's daughter, Lucy. 'Dad passed away last week. I just wanted to say thank you for talking to him last summer. It was the highlight of his year. Best wishes, Lucy.'

Grace was with Alan, her boyfriend. Man-friend. Friend then. She didn't mention the text about Billy Spottiswood. Why would she?

Alan was her third internet date. Bev was behind it. Not pushing, but just giving her a little nudge. Bev had been right, of course. You really don't know unless you try it. But it was tiring. All that meeting up, telling each other a few selected highlights, hoping he's not lying. Then the following bit. To kiss or not to kiss. Not with Number One, not with Number Two and not there yet with Number Three. And those tumbling waves would dry up before that happened.

She was trying to find a way to tell him it was over after one date, which they were currently on, post-lunch. Their only thing in common was 'The Jurassic Coast'.

She was aware of the idea that you could be comfortably silent in someone's company, but this silence was hard work – mainly because each of them continually fought to come up with an interesting comment.

"It really is quite hot," he said.

"Very hot," she agreed.

"We could do with a bit of a breeze," he added.

"Definitely," she concurred.

She had put her life right. That's what mattered. She was beginning to accept that it might be a life alone, but that was okay. At least she'd tried. And who was to say that Mr Right wouldn't unexpectedly turn up one day to prove her wrong?

Dealing with the divorce hadn't been much fun. Emptying out their stuff from the house had felt strange, as if part of herself had died and needed to be cleared away. It wasn't an all-new Grace who moved into a small flat. It was a resigned Grace.

She had kept a few things, of course. The old Lyric ledgers, the photo of Lizzie, some books…

An expensive ornamental bronze lion from a Cornish holiday with Dennis went to the charity shop though. It was a nice object, but it represented nothing.

The waves continued rolling in. That was the thing with waves. It was like the lungs of the world breathing in and out, in and out… until the end of time.

And, as she often did, she wondered…

"I wish I'd brought a hat," said Alan.

"Hmm… have you ever heard of Lesley Pearce, the marathon runner?" she asked.

"I don't think so."

"She's run three marathons since last summer."

"Oh… is that an interest of yours?"

"Running? No. It's just that Lesley's raised thousands for a diabetes charity. Isn't that incredible?"

"Yes, it is."

"That woman is making a difference to so many lives."

"Yes, she is."

Grace sighed. All thoughts of making a real difference had been put back in the box, the lid screwed down, and the wretched thing buried in a metaphorical garden.

Her phone pinged.

She checked it.

As requested, Bev was fifty yards away, by the benches at the back of the beach.

Good ol' Bev.

Grace turned to her date.

"I have to go."

"Oh, right."

"Look… I don't think this is working out. Could we just say a friendly goodbye?"

"Yes, I think it's for the best. Your profile suggested someone more interesting."

"That's two of us disappointed in me then. Goodbye, Alan."

She watched him cross the road and waited for him to be completely out of sight before she descended the beach steps to join Bev.

"Grace Chapman, you are hereby invited to come with me and shop for a new top. My treat. We'll smarten ourselves up a bit."

Grace smiled. "You already look smart."

"Hey, why look good when you can look great?"

"I'm fine, honestly."

"Are you sure? We're in our sixties, not our nineties."

"Not now, Bev. Let's have a cup of tea somewhere. I'm gasping."

"Alright, let's do that. But you ought to know a new top wouldn't be wasted. I've had a text from a mutual friend."

"Oh?"

"He's back."

Thirty-Three

Grace was comfortable in her armchair listening to Aunt Jen's crackly copy of the Beatles album, *Rubber Soul*.

She was also thinking about the past, and about Mary Smith. What must it have been like to live through those vibrant days of the early 1960s? Pop records, TV, radio, magazines… and then, sixty years later, to be living in a sheltered accommodation apartment with only the memories for company.

She glanced up at the photo of Lizzie La Grange on the mantlepiece. She had spent decades paying no attention to it at Aunt Jen's. It still felt odd to be in Lizzie's presence and know the whole story.

Next to Lizzie was a strip of four photo-booth snaps in a narrow, upright rectangular frame. Four moments in time. Ripped in half and taped back together. The photo at the top suggested uncertainty. The one at the bottom said he was the man for her.

And now he was back for a summer visit.

She felt the relief of having retrieved it that time from the waste basket, and that the rip was through the white space between the second and third photos.

The communal main door entry-phone buzzed.

It brought her back to the present.

She hesitated before answering it. What did he really want? Indeed, what did she really want? At sixty-three, it might have seemed reasonable to know the answer. After all, there was plenty of life experience there – 126 years, if you combined their ages.

"Hello?" she said into the small video screen by her front door.

"You've moved," said Russ.

"Yes, out of suburbia into a block nearer the front. Come in."

She pressed the green button, which would unlock the main door and let him in. She then opened her own front door and listened as he came along the stone-floor lobby… and then watched as he passed the stone stairway and came along the short corridor to number 12 on the ground floor.

"This is nice," he said as he came in.

"It's perfect for me," she said as she showed him to the sitting room. "I had to ditch quite a few things, but it was surprisingly okay."

Most of Aunt Jen's furniture had been affordable Victorian and Edwardian antiques, which always felt welcoming and warm. Grace had got a few of the pieces back from the second-hand dealer she'd off-loaded them to.

"It has warmth," he said, taking a seat on Aunt Jen's old Chesterfield sofa and glancing up at the mantlepiece to the array of framed photos. "Oh, look at those two!" he declared, no doubt spotting the photobooth strip. "I wonder what became of them?"

Grace took a seat in the armchair opposite him. Now they had a coffee table between them, but no coffee.

"I keep old things sometimes. I form an attachment."

He squinted at the strip.

"Did you tear it in half?"

"I did, but I mended it. You can do that with old things."

"Well, as I say, it's a lovely flat."

"Thanks. I kept some of Aunt Jen's stuff. It's important to me. I just didn't know it at the time."

"Good ol' Aunt Jen. Let's not forget she liked me and said I wasn't a crazed psycho."

"She always was a terrible judge of character."

Russ laughed.

"Well, it's a lovely home, Grace. I can see you're happy here."

"I am," she said with a smile. Elm Court, a late-Victorian red brick block of flats, wasn't dissimilar to

Crowthorne Court where her aunt had lived for fifty years. Situated near Aunt Jen's old flat and Bev's place too, it really did feel like home.

"A fresh start then," said Russ.

"Yes… I've learned a lot about myself this past year."

"Good for you. I hope you've learned that you're a lovely person and a great friend."

"I have, thanks to Bev telling me a thousand times."

"Good ol' Bev. Did she mention there's a man who doesn't feel happy without you?"

"No, she didn't. In fact, no one's mentioned that."

"Well… let me say a bit more."

"The thing is, by being free of relationships, I've learned to be… what's the word?"

"Miserable?"

"Independent."

"You're the best, Grace. You really are. I can see you're not happy with me, but it doesn't change anything. You're a fabulous, funny, friendly, loving, giving person. I know I've helped to mess things up between us, but I hope you have a few fond memories of me. It wasn't all bad, was it."

Grace wasn't sure what to say or do. Was this the moment she showed him out or the moment she dragged him close and kissed him, accepting that a fling would be enough?

In the end, she said and did nothing, leaving him to get to his feet.

"Well, I ought to be…"

She followed him the door, which he opened, meaning he was neither in nor out of her life for just this moment.

"It's a shame we weren't able to put that show on," he said.

Ah… neutral ground. Good!

"Yes, about that. Last year I took a chance. I booked the Lyric for this year. A million-to-one shot, I know, but I booked it anyway."

"Wow. Really?"

"Yes, really."

"So, it's on then. At least, it could be if we put the whole thing together again."

"Well… why don't you come back in. We could have some coffee and discuss it."

He smiled as he stepped back into her life.

"Grace, you have to admit, it was mad last year – trying to get it all done in, what, three weeks?"

"Yes, well, this time it would be one."

"One?"

"The booking's for next week."

Russ laughed with mild panic.

"You know, I must get my ears tested. For a second there, I thought you said *next week*."

Thirty-Four

Grace was on Mary's doorstep, smiling into a confused face.

"It's lovely to see you, Grace," said Mary, showing her in. "Is everything alright?"

"Yes, fine. How are you?"

"The same as I was when you were here yesterday. Are you sure everything's alright?"

"It is. More than that – I'm feeling inspired."

"Hmm, that sounds dangerous."

"Let's have some tea and I'll tell you all about it."

A few minutes later, they were seated in the main living area with tea and biscuits.

"You remember the Harmony Festival?" said Grace.

"Yes, I haven't lost my faculties. What about it?"

"It's on."

"On? How do you mean?"

"The show… it's on. Next week, to be exact."

"Next week? That's… nuts. You haven't bashed your head, have you?"

"No, I haven't. The show is on, and I'd like you to be a part of it."

Mary slumped just a little.

"I don't know, Grace. I'm getting too old to perform for a crowd."

"Well, think about it. There's no rush."

"No rush?"

"Obviously, seven days is a kind of rush, theatrically-speaking… I mean just let me know by tomorrow."

"Right, well… is it for the same charity?"

"Yes, the Carpenter-Ford Music Charity. The one Russ found last year."

"Is that what's provoked this? Russ?"

"In a way, yes. I actually made the booking last year. You know, being stupidly optimistic. Anyway, Russ is back, and I thought – why not?"

"I see. You know, I think you two could be happy together."

"I don't know. I'm just trying to get a show on at the Lyric and Russ is helping me with it. That's all."

"That's the trouble with being old. Practical reasons spoil everything. When we're young and passionate, we race into things. No questions."

A silence unexpectedly followed, in which Grace wondered if they were thinking the same thing.

"Tell me about my real dad," she asked.

Without a word, Mary went to a drawer in the side cabinet and retrieved the photo booth strip of two young people. She handed it to Grace.

"Where did he go? America, wasn't it?"

"No, it was another part of London."

"Oh… not America?"

"I made that up. A friend said they thought he'd gone to share a flat with a girlfriend in Kilburn."

Grace studied the photos more closely.

"I look like you, not him."

Mary gave a sad smile. "I'm still sure you think badly of me."

Grace recalled a moment on a warm September evening at the beach, and Russ having something important to tell her.

"My teen story's no different to yours, Mary. I thought Russ was going to suggest we get serious. I saw marriage on the horizon. In my head and heart, I'd already given myself to him. In life though, on the verge of us taking that next step, he left for Manchester."

Mary considered it for a moment.

"Life has its way," she said. "Would you like to know your real father's name?"

"No. Tell me about Jimmy."

"Really?"

"Yes."

"Oh, my lovely Jimmy was the real deal, thank God. We had so many wonderful years together. He was a loving man with a lovely sense of humour, and I miss him every day."

Mary went on to describe how Jimmy had worked at a film processing workshop, from junior assistant to senior manager, dealing with overnight rushes from the movie business at Pinewood Studios. Mary, herself, had worked behind numerous department store perfume counters.

The memories continued for some time – in fact, until it was time for a second cuppa.

"So… the show," Mary eventually said, bringing them around full circle.

"Yes, the show. I do hope you can be part of it. Just for one performance. To give people a taste of what it was like."

Mary considered it for a moment and then broke into a broad smile.

"You can call me Coco."

"Brilliant."

"I'll let my sisters know it's on."

"Absolutely. We definitely want all three of you."

Coco-Mary went back to the drawer and retrieved something else.

"You might want this," she said, handing it over.

It was the sheet music for 'Seize the Day'.

"You found it!" said Grace.

"No, I sent away for it. Sentimental reasons."

"Well, now we've got it for practical reasons. Russ didn't bring his copy with him."

Thirty-Five

Grace and Russ were seated at her dining table, watching a video on her laptop. It was the Swinging Sixties Band, a tribute outfit playing at a birthday bash in Torquay. What's more, the band was led by Russ's friend from way back, Chrissie Miles.

"They're good," said Grace.

"And they're all yours. There's a list of songs on their website. You just pick the ones you want."

"Great."

After the video, Grace pulled up the Carpenter-Ford Music Charity website on her phone. There was something that had been bugging her.

"It's a music charity helping young people," she said.

"Yes, it is."

"Then couldn't we have some young musicians as part of the show?"

"Yes, a good idea – but I doubt there's time to get anything arranged."

"I wonder if any local schools have an orchestra?"

"I'm sure they do, but it's the summer holidays."

"Hmm… what if we could get, say, three of four brass players. They could do something simple, like back a singer for one song. A song you're playing at the piano. A few simple notes."

"Yes, it's do-able if you find the right kids."

"The Carpenter-Ford Music Charity could find them for us. They'd know who would be up to playing on stage. I'll get onto it."

"Great," said Russ. "Now, what about VIP guests?"

Grace handed him a long list of names.

Russ frowned. "Have you invited all these?"

"Only those marked with an X."

"Five?"

"You think I need more?"

"The Bald Eagles… you haven't marked them."

"It's a comedy band. I wasn't sure."

"If you get one of them along, you might get a funny anecdote you could incorporate into the show… and you'll certainly have a good laugh afterwards."

"Alright."

Russ mused. "Young and old in harmony. I like it. And I reckon the local newspaper will like it too."

"How about calling it the Harmony Festival Charity Bash?" Grace wondered.

"Hey, that sounds good to me," said Russ.

*

"Hello, sir? Hello?"

Grace let the man walk past before turning to the next passer-by.

"Hello? I wonder if you'd be interested in coming to a charity concert in aid of… no?"

She and Russ were in the town centre handing out flyers to holidaymakers. They had only been at it for a few minutes, but Grace wasn't happy.

"I think we need to hone our approach."

"Agreed. I thought they'd stop and listen."

Just then, a third activist arrived.

"Hello!" said Russ.

"Sorry, I'm late" said Bev. "I bumped into a neighbour."

"Thanks for coming," said Grace. "We seem to be having a problem with our sales pitch."

Russ nodded. "Stopping people is harder than we thought."

Bev gave a little shrug. "Aren't you forgetting something? My dad ran a nick-nack stall in the market for thirty years. I used to help him on Saturday mornings."

With the memory racing back to her, Grace turned to Russ.

"It's true, she did."

They watched Bev swing into action with an approaching middle-aged couple who wore the relaxed look of tourists.

"Special offer! The best show in town has bargain ticket prices. And guess what, all the profits are going to an amazing children's charity!"

The couple stopped.

Grace turned to Russ and they both laughed.

Bev then informed the couple about the charity and the show.

"Two tickets?" she was saying a moment later. She theatrically pointed to the flyer she had given them. "Yes, indeed, just use the magic of your phone to whizz over to the Shawcross Lyric Theatre website and follow the simple instructions to purchase your tickets. And before you do, can I just say thank you on behalf of all those grateful children. You're making a difference to their lives."

Russ nudged Grace. "Watch and learn."

By one o'clock they had handed out hundreds of flyers and only had to pick up a dozen or so that people had dropped or tossed away.

"Any idea how many tickets we've sold?" Russ asked.

"Well, we've had a hundred promises…" said Grace. She checked the website. "… and thirty-two sales. I reckon a few of those promises will convert over the lunch period when people have a bit of time."

"Great stuff," said Bev. "If we can double it after lunch, we'll be getting somewhere."

Grace felt a dose of realism wouldn't hurt.

"Let's not forget the Lyric holds 520. That's a lot of people."

"It is, but let's be positive," said Bev. "Let's visualize a great afternoon selling lots of tickets."

Grace smiled. "Alright, we'll do that."

"Lunch first?" Russ suggested.

"Now you're talking," said Bev.

They found a café where they could sit outside with a sandwich and a cold apple juice apiece.

While they ate, Grace wondered if she was making a mistake in not telling Russ how she felt. Perhaps she would tell him later when the opportunity arose.

Russ meanwhile was busy musing. "I wonder how many backsides on seats they've had there over the years. At the Lyric, I mean."

"No idea," said Bev. "It'll be 520 seats times a million years."

"Almost," said Russ. "During the summer… matinees and evenings, although possibly not all full houses…" He switched to the calculator on his phone. "Plus, out-of-season numbers…"

"Mainly Fridays and Saturdays," said Grace, "and a few midweek concerts."

Russ tapped in some numbers then looked up.

"And multiply all that by what – a hundred years?"

"More or less," said Grace.

"What do we get?" asked Bev.

Russ raised an eyebrow. "Just over ten million."

"Wow," said Grace. "That's a lot of people."

"Yep," said Russ, "getting another few hundred suddenly doesn't seem such a big number."

Ten minutes later, they were back on their feet, with Grace and Russ watching whirlwind Bev storm off into the fray.

Grace smiled.

"She's brilliant, isn't she."

"Yes, she is."

"Russ? Thanks for all your help with this."

"No problem. I'm sure it'll be a storming success. Just don't forget to text me with updates on the day."

Grace felt a mild shock.

"Are you not coming?"

"No, you've got all the bases covered."

"Yes, I have, but…"

"I'm staying with my aunt for a few days then I'll be heading off on Monday. I'll make a contribution on the Just Giving page though. Is fifty pounds okay?"

"That would be great. Thanks. So, your train is on show day?"

"Yes, just before midday. At 11.47, to be exact. That's to say, I want to catch the 11.47 train to Newton Abbot to make the connection to York."

"You've already booked it?"

"Yes."

"Any reason for not staying?"

"It was the plan all along. I mean I had no idea you'd booked the theatre. I just thought if I could help a friend, then I would. You've got comedians, a band… you'll figure it out."

"I'll be without a pianist."

"Chrissie Miles from the Swinging Sixties Band plays piano. I've already updated him on what you need."

"Right, so that just leaves the after-show party in the bar."

Russ shook his head.

"You'll be high on adrenalin and success, and everyone's going have a well-earned drink or three. I don't think me being there for a party would be a good idea."

Grace nodded. He was right Their ill-matched lives didn't need an opportunity to stir up emotions that weren't buried all that deep.

"Right… well… that's everything covered then, Russ."

"Yep – now let's fill the place to the rafters."

She wondered if this might be a good time to tell him she loved him despite the difficulties. But he turned and walked off waving flyers at people. And that, apparently, was that.

Thirty-Six

Grace was approaching the Shawcross Lyric, which these days was a mere five-minute walk from her flat. The Harmony Festival Charity Bash was due to get under way in – she checked her watch – just a couple of hours, but she could already feel the excitement and trepidation building. The success of the entire venture was within reach as long as nothing went wrong.

What was that saying? If something *can* go wrong, it *will* go wrong.

Actually, was it a saying? Or was it some ancient law?

No, it would be fine. She had local comedian Henry Cass to act as Master of Ceremonies and another comedian, Willy West, to do a single five-minute spot. Then she had the Swinging Sixties Band and the Three Cocos. She also had Sarah, Meera and Tim, three local youth players, who would add brass to Coco's hit.

The stage door was round the side, where performers could park their cars and large vehicles could deliver equipment. Grace went in via the main entrance though, where a few people were milling around.

She smiled. Yes, it was an architectural confusion outside, but inside it was almost perfect. Over to the left, she glanced to where the side extension housed the educational facilities, chamber music space, bar, Sea View Café, and the outside terrace. But she went the other way, through a side door, down some stairs, and through the old part of the theatre to arrive backstage.

She immediately spotted a familiar face.

"Is everyone here, Bev?"

"And good morning to you too, Grace."

"Sorry, getting anxious. There doesn't seem to be anyone here though."

"We said ten-thirty. It's currently just after ten."

Grace checked her watch again. "Right."

Bev gave a little frown.

"You're worrying too much."

Grace wasn't sure how to reply. How much was too much?

Maybe I'm not worrying enough!

"I wish Russ could be here."

"Don't say that. You've got everything covered."

Grace smiled. "Thanks, Bev. For everything."

"No problem."

"Actually, could you see if anyone's at the stage door?"

"Sure thing."

As soon as Bev had gone, Grace looked for another task.

Audience?

She peeped out from the wings. The hall was empty. Of course it was! The show didn't start for nearly two hours. Relieved, she checked the printed schedule.

THE HARMONY FESTIVAL CHARITY BASH
Schedule.

12.00: Henry Cass MC. 5 mins opening.

12.05: Swinging Sixties. 5x Beatles medley.

12.18: Henry. 3 mins.

12.21: Swinging Sixties. 5x Stones medley.

12.34. Henry. 1 min.

12.35. Willy West. 5 mins comedy.

12.40. Henry. 1 min.

12.41. Swinging Sixties. 5x Various medley.

12.54. Henry. 3 mins.

12.57: Charity mention. Hello VIPs.

1.00: Henry 1 min. Intro Cocos.

1.01: Swinging Sixties, Cocos. 2x 60s songs.

1.07: Swinging Sixties, Cocos, brass. Seize the Day.

1.10: Henry. 2 mins to close.

1.12: ALL. Singalong medley 60s hits.

1.25: Finish.

"All going well?" Judy, the manager asked, appearing in the corridor.

"We're all good, thanks." Grace then talked her through the line-up and even mentioned the library of material she was gathering on the old performers.

With Judy then heading away to her duties, Grace checked her watch and wondered if to text Russ, perhaps to ask if he'd reconsider doing Seize the Day with the Cocos.

Or would that come across as a desperate-sounding request?

*

Grace checked her watch. The show was due to start in forty-five minutes and the band had yet to turn up. Despite feeling queasy, she put on a brave smile for VIP guests Sheila Carpenter and Maggie Ford, the retired music teacher and magistrate who had set up the Carpenter-Ford Music Charity. These lovely seniors were with Sheila's daughter, Theresa, who effectively ran it.

"It's very exciting," said Sheila.

"We're ever so grateful," said Maggie.

"Sorry to invade backstage," said Theresa. "They wanted to have peek behind the curtains."

"It's no problem at all," said Grace through a rictus grin.

"We'll leave you to it," said Theresa.

Grace watched them go and looked around. Bev's husband Jez, wearing a crisp white shirt, was needlessly adjusting his yellow kipper tie and generally loitering with nothing much to do.

"Have you seen the band?" she asked him.

"I'll have a look around," he said, which failed to boost her confidence.

Grace headed for the Green Room where performers could relax and chat until needed. Inside, she found three young brass players and two comedians. They all looked to her, perhaps expecting an update, but she just smiled and left again.

"The band?" she asked Jez in the corridor.

"No sign of them. It's probably the traffic."

Grace nodded and texted band leader Chrissie Miles. She then went to the stage door, where a young staff member was waiting to admit the right people based on the info on her handheld screen. Grace smiled then turned and headed for the foyer to greet the other VIP guests, as arranged.

"How's it going?" asked Suzanne Dawson, the former lead singer of the 1960s group, the Rag Dolls. She looked great in a black and white zig-zag dress.

"Oh, fine, fine… thanks for coming, Suzanne."

"Thanks for asking us," said 1970s cabaret singer, Felicity Berlin, looking cool in a black blouse.

"Well, it's wonderful to see you," Grace enthused. "Now, let's get you a drink at the bar. And please take these."

She handed them a paper ticket each for front row seats.

The two minutes it took to get them coffee at the bar seemed to take half an hour. Then, as she left them to enjoy their hot drinks, her phone buzzed. It was a text from Chrissie Miles.

She read it and turned wide-eyed to Bev, who had come to look for her.

"Grace?"

"This cannot be happening."

Bev's brow furrowed. "Not the band?"

Grace could only nod.

"Text him back," said Bev. "Offer him money."

Grace did so, although it was hard to type as her blood had turned to ice. She and Bev then stared at Grace's phone for the next minute or so.

Her messages updated.

'Sorry. In Birmingham last night. Finished late. Stayed over and now have transport problem. Could poss get to you by three?'

Grace typed a reply. 'We start in 30 mins.'

"We need a new plan," said Bev.

But Grace was still furious with Chrissie.

"A Sunday gig? I don't believe him."

She phoned him.

"Chrissie? What's going on."

"Um… okay… honest truth. I've just finished a corporate weekend. Me and our drummer work for the same firm. Lots of drinks last night. Boy…"

"I don't believe this. How could you?"

"Really sorry. We're on a train to Exeter. Sorry to have lied to you. Bad form."

"Oh, Chrissie, you've pretty much destroyed the show."

"Ouch. Sorry again. I told Russ it should be okay. I mean we're working from home today, so I assumed we could have slipped out for a few hours. It's just that we're still a long way from home. I don't suppose you have a back-up plan?"

Grace huffed and ended the call.

"He wonders if we have a back-up plan."

"Perhaps Fate has one?" Bev said through stricken features.

"We're stuck," said Grace. "Absolutely, totally stuck. It couldn't be any worse."

"Um…" Bev seemed ready to deliver more bad news.

"What is it?"

"Isn't the guy from the Torbay Echo due soon?"

Thirty-Seven

"Grace Chapman?" It was an elderly chap approaching the bar. "A man called Jez pointed me in this direction."

"Oh…" Grace tried to work out who he was. He seemed a little old to be working for the Echo. "It's not Steve, is it?"

"That's right, Steve Reid plus two reporting for VIP duty. Do we get pampered with champers and served oysters? Sorry, just joking."

Grace tried to smile but she felt sick.

"No, no, come on over. Let me get you a beer or a coffee."

Steve came over, followed by two friends of a similar vintage.

"This is Fred and Dave," said Steve. "We think it's a marvellous thing you're doing."

"Well, thank you for coming. Please use these tickets. You've got very good seats. Now, coffee, beer?"

"Just one thing," said Steve. "It's a bit cheeky…"

"Yes?"

"Well, as the Bald Eagles, we still perform. Now I know we're here as VIP guests, and we're very grateful. It's just that we have a banjo, a guitar, and a snare drum in the car, and plenty of songs ready to go. Would anyone be offended if we entertained people by the bar? It would just be a little bit of fun. You know, add a touch of musical comedy before the show starts. Fifteen minutes, max. What do you think…?"

Grace felt tears forming, so she gave a little laugh and brushed them away.

"Steve, Fred, Dave… I have a much, much better suggestion."

*

Grace, Bev and Jez were still reeling from the turn of events. The Bald Eagles would perform more than just a comedy song or two and things needed to be re-jigged. However, the Three Cocos had emerged from their dressing rooms wearing matching sparkly gowns and wanted to know what was happening.

"A banjo?" said Coco-Mary. "I'll practise with a kazoo player, but I usually perform with a pianist or an orchestra."

"Just have a seat in the Green Room, please. I'll think of something."

They did so, but with a fuss.

"Now what?" said Jez. "Is Russ an option? The house piano's already on stage."

"Unfortunately, no," said Bev.

Grace checked her watch.

"He'll be at the station about now."

"Could you text him?"

"I already did – ages ago. No reply. Maybe his phone's switched off."

"Bev or me could drive you there," said Jez. "If that helps?"

"Did you park by the stage door?"

"No, I didn't want take up performers' spaces, so I used the council car park."

Grace grimaced. "That's in the opposite direction to the station."

"It's only a five-minute walk… plus paying and getting out and driving to the station. Ten, twelve minutes?"

"Sorry, Jez. I could get there quicker on foot."

Bev gasped. "Then what are you waiting for?"

"You're right. We need Russ to play Seize the Day. After all, Coco Vincenza is the most significant three persons in the theatre. I'll have to run."

"Wow, you're going to run?"

"Yes."

She understood Bev's look, but raced off as fast as she could.

At eighteen, Bev had been genuinely impressed at her letting him leave without a care – when in fact she'd run all the way to station to spy on him, and to make sure it really was the end of the world.

For the all-new, sixty-three-year-old Grace, it seemed ridiculous to be hurrying. She'd seen movies like this, where the hero races across town to stop their true love getting on the plane, boat, helicopter, space rocket or, in her case, the 11.47 train to Newton Abbot which would give a timely connection for the onward journey to York.

Of course, most of the films she loved were from the 50s, 60s, 70s and 80s, and pre-dated pinging a text to a smart phone. This was the 21st century though, and she had indeed pinged a text saying, 'Not too late to do Seize the Day with the Cocos?' – which just went to show that people could still be unreachable if they wanted to be.

She came to a halt a hundred yards short of the station, puffing hard and sweating, and wishing she could swap legs with Lesley Pearce.

He hadn't answered though, so why chase him? Indeed, what would he think of a crazed, gasping senior citizen begging him to come back.

That said, perhaps there was a compromise between hurrying and not bothering. She could walk the rest of the way. Then she could say she was idly passing the station and thought she'd see if he was okay… and he'd no doubt say his phone was switched off or his battery had packed up.

She began walking…

…until fear of being too late took over again and she began speed walking, just like in the Olympics where they look like they might throw a hip joint at any moment.

But the fear continued to increase, so she sprinted the last thirty yards to arrive at the barrier with the train pulling away.

Defeat.

But Grace only allowed that sentiment to reside there for a few moments, at which point she took a fortifying breath and stood up straight. This didn't have to be a loss. With a bit of last-minute re-thinking, it could yet be a triumph of the three Cocos singing unaccompanied, just like that time on the bus.

Yes, there were doubts – millions of them – but she refused to listen to them as she hurried all the way back to the theatre, arriving horribly breathless and a little dizzy.

"I don't suppose… he doubled back?" she gasped.

"No," said Bev, looking worried.

Grace raced to the side of the stage and peeked out. The theatre was almost full of happy holidaymakers.

Oh my…

She turned and almost bumped into Judy, the manager, who was wearing a worried professional smile.

"Is everything alright?"

"Yes," said Grace, still breathing hard. "Yes… we'll start and finish on time, don't worry."

"Perfect. It's just that, um… your drummer seems a little short of kit."

"Ah, yes… I'm sure he can bash his snare drum quite loudly though."

Judy smiled. "The best thing about showbiz is how people rally round when things get difficult. We've had a band here for a couple of weeks as part of the summer show. I'm sure they won't miss a few drums and cymbals for a couple of hours. It's all tucked away in the store if someone wants to get it…?"

"Oh, thank you, Judy, thank you…"

Grace was still smiling as Judy and the Bald Eagles went off to arrange it.

"One minute to showtime," said Jez, somewhat unhelpfully.

Grace nodded and attempted to embrace the challenge.

"Right then… Seize the Day. The Three Cocos can sing it acapella… no music…"

"Good idea," said Bev. "I don't suppose they could do Abba too? I was thinking of 'Thank You For The Music'. We could dedicate it to Russ and Chrissie."

"Let's focus on the here and now," said Grace. "So, that's Henry on first… then the Bald Eagles, who I'm now in love with, then the second comedian, then a bit more Henry before I do the VIPs and a charity talk. We'll finish with a singalong."

"Right."

Grace felt hollow. "It's not enough for a whole show, is it."

Bev looked down at the floor. "Probably not, no, but it'll have to do."

Just then, they heard someone onstage at the piano.

They were playing 'How Deep Is Your Love'.

Thirty-Eight

Grace and Bev hurried to the wings. He was onstage playing beautifully.

Grace smiled. And then she surprised herself by singing quietly along with it.

Bev nudged her.

"You have to admit, he has a certain style."

He finished playing to polite applause, which prompted Grace to check her watch. It was just after midday. She looked round to find Henry Cass at her side.

"What's the plan?" he asked.

Grace thought for a second.

"The plan is… you stay there for a minute."

Grace walked out onto the stage to an expectant audience. She nodded to Russ, still seated at the piano and smiled bravely at the crowd. It was hard to see with the stage lights shining at her, but there in the front row were Sheila, Maggie and Theresa… and Suzanne Dawson, who appeared on this very stage several times between 1965 and 1967… and cabaret singer, Felicity Berlin, who appeared a dozen times between 1973 and 1975.

Grace took a breath.

"Hello," she squeaked. She gave a little cough to clear her throat and then belted out the follow up. "Welcome to the Shawcross Lyric!"

There was a muted cheer from the crowd.

"Today, we're celebrating the rich history of entertainment here at the Lyric. We've had some big names in the past – Max Bygraves, Bruce Forsyth, Lulu – but you know, without talented artists such as Suzanne Dawson of the Rag Dolls, cabaret singer Felicity Berlin, and the comedian, Billy Spottiswood, who we sadly lost recently, the Lyric wouldn't have been able to entertain over *ten million* happy customers since its doors first opened in 1920."

A small round of applause rippled through the hall.

"A little confession now. The original band we booked couldn't make it at the *very last minute*. But we have put together something really special for you. You've already met a lovely man, a generous soul, someone you can rely on, who will never let you down… Russ Adams!"

Russ looked left, right and behind him… and then pointed a finger at himself, comedy-style.

"Me?"

The audience laughed generously.

Grace went on. "Today's show is in support of a wonderful cause – the Carpenter-Ford Music Charity. We'll tell you a bit more about their work later, but now, without further ado, please welcome the lovely, the wonderful… Henry Cass."

Henry bowled onto the stage, nodding to Grace and Russ as they passed him on their way off.

"Hello, hello!" he declared. "It's good to see you all here today. Thank you for coming. Now, does anyone enjoy flamenco dancing? No? Just me? Well, you might be surprised to know I had lessons last summer. Well, when I say lessons, I was asked to leave halfway through the first one…"

While the audience began to chuckle along with Henry's anecdote, Grace, Bev, Russ and Jez gathered together backstage.

"The piano intro?" Grace queried.

Russ shrugged. "The manager told me the band had failed to turn up, so I went into the hall and…well… the audience were there, and it was already twelve. I thought of coming to find out what was going on, but the spotlight was on the piano. I don't know what I was thinking, to be honest."

"I'm just glad you're here," said Grace.

"If you'd told me about the band in your text, I'd have been here sooner."

"I didn't know when I texted. I mean I didn't want you reading a second text on the train and having the transport police explain it's not a valid reason for pulling the emergency cord."

"Let's get this show sorted," said Bev. "We can talk later."

"Do you have any kind of schedule?" Russ asked.

"Yes, but it probably needs another re-jig," said Jez.

Grace took a breath. "Right… off the top of my head… we'll have a singalong next."

Russ looked worried. "My singalong repertoire's limited, to say the least."

"No, the Bald Eagles know the music to tons of sixties songs. They'll do all the singalongs."

Russ's worried look turn to puzzlement. "Er…?"

"All you need know is they're here and a lot of their comedy songs are based on well-known 60s and 70s tunes. As long as we print off the genuine lyrics for them and maybe put them on the big screen too…"

"I could do that," said Jez.

"Great, then we'll have more from Henry… then another singalong. Then Willy West… then a word about the charity and our VIPS. Um… then Henry… then the Bald Eagles can do a comedy song… then we'll have the Three Cocos for Seize the Day with you, Russ. We'll bring on the brass with a proper introduction for them."

"It's in a slow, simple 3:4 time," said Russ. "The Bald Eagles' drummer could come in with the brass for the final verse and chorus. I'll have a word with him."

"Perfect. Then we'll have Henry work the audience up for a final singalong with the band. The rest of us can be onstage and give our tonsils a workout. How does that sound?"

"A bit short?" said Jez.

Bev shoved him. "It sounds bloody brilliant. Let's do it."

Thirty-Nine

As the final chorus of the final singalong ended with vigorous applause, Grace felt an elation beyond all her sixty-three years on earth. She was shattered and possibly slightly delirious, but they had done it.

While she blinked away a few justified tears, Coco-Mary leaned into the microphone.

"I could tell you all some backstage stories…"

"No, you can't," said Grace into another mic. "We'd be sued."

The crowd laughed.

Grace was caught off-guard. She'd never made 442 people laugh before.

"Well, in the pub later then," said Coco-Carol.

This caused more laughter.

And Grace laughed too.

It was finally, *finally* over.

Except it wasn't. Coco-Carol and Coco-Linda moved alongside and raised Grace's arms aloft, while Coco-Mary had one last thing to say.

"Ladies and Gentlemen, please show your appreciation for our ringleader, Grace Chapman, the woman who gets things done!"

The crowd cheered and applauded generously.

Grace blushed. And her heart certainly thumped. But she felt thrilled. And more tears rolled down her cheeks.

"Thank you!" was all she could say.

"Bye all!" cried Coco-Carol. "And thank you for coming!"

And that was that. People were getting to their feet and leaving the auditorium in what seemed to be a happy mood. Grace watched most of them go before she wandered out the back to hug lots of people. She then went to the stage door and stood outside for some much-needed fresh air. Her thoughts, of course, were all over the place.

We did it…. ha-ha! We actually did it!

Russ came out to join her.

"Hey… you are brilliant. I knew you could do it."

"Thanks, Russ, but it was team effort."

"Absolutely. This kind of thing was always going to need great people working on it. I'm not including me in that, by the way."

"Thanks for coming back. Honestly, we couldn't have done it without you."

"Yes, about that…"

"I texted you."

"Yes, you did."

"You didn't answer."

"No, sorry about that. I was going to text you back right away, you know, to say goodbye. Then I wondered if that was the right thing to do. So, I went for a long walk and thought about it. Then I headed here thinking if I didn't text, I could still change my mind and get the next train. That was a possibility right up until I stepped onto the stage." He sighed. "I'm really sorry to have messed you around. You don't deserve that. I was just being a bit of a coward about… you know."

"What?"

"Well… I was by the sea wall… and I had a choice. Get on the train and have a simple life or come to the theatre and have a crazy upside-down few months while I sort out a shedload of life stuff…"

Grace smiled. "Big decisions."

"Yes, big decisions. It's like we've known each other all our lives, apart from a tiny four-decade gap that doesn't seem so big right now."

"I feel the same. When you left…"

"The first or second time?"

She shoved him playfully.

"The first time. I told myself it was just a silly infatuation, nothing more. When I met Dennis, I was so ready to commit. Last year, when he came back, I told myself I'd make my marriage work. If I'm being honest, I seem to have a habit of getting it wrong, and that's still my worry."

"Okay, well, when I left the first time… I did come back before you were married."

"What?"

"I saw you and Dennis together at the White Lion one Friday night. It was really busy and I was over on one side with a few mates. You were on the other side. I almost came over to say hello, but you looked so *right* together. I was glad you were getting a happy-ever-after. So, you're not alone in getting it wrong."

"Well, life has its own plan, I'm sure. Just don't ask me what it is."

"Don't ask me either, but there's an opportunity here for us."

"To draw a line, you mean?"

"Well, a line with little gaps in it. A line that says the past is behind us and the future is the thing now."

"What are the little gaps for?"

"They're to let the good memories come through."

"I see."

"I don't want to lose our past. I don't want to lose our future either."

"So, the life stuff, the big decisions… you sound like you want us to be together."

"I love you, Grace. I've always loved you, apart from that forty-odd-year gap. I'm sorry I never told you last year.

I'm telling you now though and I'm hoping it's not too late."

Grace's heart swelled with emotion, which was difficult to suppress.

"Russ, we're in our sixties and we're both settled in different parts of the country. A few days or weeks together isn't enough. That's been the problem all along."

"I know, but what if we changed the plan."

"How?"

"By making things permanent."

Grace wanted exactly that, but she still wasn't sure.

"I'm nervous because I'd be placing all of me into this."

"I won't let you down, Grace. Never."

"I love you, Russ. I've always loved you. I just had to forget it so I could get on with my life."

He leaned forward… and they kissed, soft and slow. It was just a few seconds, but it meant everything.

"Grace? I assume you'll be putting on another show next year?" he asked, their faces still close.

"I will."

"I expect we'll be married by then."

She would have answered him right away, but her eyes had filled up and her heart was thumping.

She swallowed and composed herself.

"Yes, I expect we will. Probably around May. Or would you prefer June?"

"I think you should decide. You're brilliant at arranging things."

Judy Frost, the manager appeared, and they pulled apart.

"Ah, there you are. Congratulations. That was lovely. A real triumph and a great success for the charity, I'm sure."

"Thank you so much for everything," said Grace. "You've been so helpful."

"All part of the service. Now, there's something I'd like to discuss when you have a moment. I'm a big fan of the Lyric's history, which has given me an idea."

Forty

The sky was blue over Shawcross beach. The few small clouds were white and fluffy. A gentle breeze ruffled Grace Chapman's salt and pepper locks while, just ahead, a succession of breaking waves raced in and threatened to cover her sandals. She kept back though. She wouldn't be having wet feet today.

A year had passed since she stood in the exact same spot to scatter Aunt Jen's ashes over the water and say farewell to the last of the older generation. Only, things had turned out to be a little more complex since then.

She looked around. On a hot August day, the holidaymakers were out in force, enjoying the South Devon seaside. There were people in deckchairs, and some playing with beachballs. A wasp flew past, no doubt in search of someone's ice cream or sweet cola drink.

Grace turned to face the sea and the horizon, to say goodbye one last time to Aunt Jen and Mum Olive.

"We finally gave the good old days a proper send-off, didn't we? I hope you liked it."

The crashing waves seemed to say yes – at least, that's what it sounded like.

"The Harmony Festival will be back next August. I've booked three successive Wednesday lunchtimes, and we'll grab a big name from one of the summer shows to open it for us."

The waves seemed to like that too.

"There's also going to be a whole bunch of people remembered every day. I hope you approve."

She thought of Billy Spottiswood.

In all, Grace was on target to collect a dozen stories to be presented as video or audio with photos in a permanent display at the Shawcross Lyric Theatre. A brand-new History Corner was in the pipeline and would be housed between the educational facilities and the Sea View Café. Alongside the audio-visual screens would be glass cabinets showcasing the theatre's own treasure trove of signed celebrity photos, programmes, and promotional materials gathered over the past century. There would also be space in a display cabinet for a pile of six ledgers, the top one being open on the page showing Coco's entry and explaining how it sparked an annual charity fundraising initiative.

With endless school visits and people gathering for lunch and afternoon tea, the voices of the past would continue to be heard, whether that be performers' stories or the Three Cocos performing 'Seize The Day'. All this would be in the theatre for the next hundred years. They wouldn't be forgotten.

Grace left the shoreline and tramped across the shingle to the benches at the back of the beach. Here, the new 'old guard' were waiting for her. Mary, Linda and Carol. There was also her best friend Bev and hubby Jez, and a husband-to-be for Grace too. She hugged them all, although it soon settled on herself and just one other.

"Hey, stand back," said Carol. "Give the romantic youngsters some space."

Everyone backed off, leaving just Grace and Russ facing each other. They were momentarily interrupted by a small boy chasing a beach ball, but he was gone in a trice.

"Kiss him then," Carol urged. She was waiting to capture the moment with a phone photo.

Grace laughed. Carol was her new daft auntie. Linda was her more sensible aunt. And Mary… well, there was a great deal more between them. Of course, she'd get to see all three for coffee mornings, lunches, and the occasional trip to the library. And they'd be VIP guests at next year's shows.

"We're still waiting," said Carol.

Grace kissed Russ. After forty-five years, their romance was complete. As some wise person surely once said, better late than never.

Grace was beginning a new life now. She had learned that people can make a difference in so many ways – from working behind the scenes, by supporting others, and, yes, by coming up with big ideas and seeing them through. Most of all though, she had learned that the truest sense of fulfilment comes to those who have found their place in the world.

"Thank you all," she said. "Thank you, Bev and Jez. Thank you, Mum Olive and Aunt Jen. Thank you, Russ. And thank you, Coco Vincenza, Coco Vincenza, and last but not least, Coco Vincenza."

Everyone laughed.

Then Aunt Carol grabbed a hunky passer-by and got him to take a group photo. All Grace could think was – *I'm going to need a bigger mantlepiece.*

As they headed off to the Sunny Side Up Café for lunch, Bev caught up with her.

"I meant to say… I overheard someone at the concert yesterday. She was talking about volunteering to help with reading at her son's junior school."

"That's great."

"She said she'd been thinking about it, but you inspired her to get started in actually doing it."

"Me?"

"Yes, you. It's called making a difference."

Grace almost laughed.

"Let me stop you there. Lesley Pearce the marathon runner is our inspiration. If it wasn't for her, I'd never have got started. She's the one who's made a difference."

"Well, between you and me, Lesley was inspired by her ten-year-old great niece, Lauren, who swam a hundred lengths of the Shawcross pool to raise money for a guide dog charity."

"Right… I see… I wonder who inspired Lauren?"

It then struck Grace, like sunshine breaking through clouds, that thanks to those who had paved the way, she could inspire endless others, which, in itself, was an inspiring thought.

*

After an enjoyable light lunch, Grace and Russ bade everyone farewell – for now. Then they headed back to the beach.

There, she took his hand as they strolled across the shingle and sand on the shoreline, oblivious to holidaymakers. They had a plan now – an exciting one as far as Grace was concerned. She would spend term time with him in York, and he'd spend the school holidays with her in Shawcross. And then, when he retired, they would decide where to make their home.

They covered a hundred yards or so to reach a quieter stretch of beach before Russ spoke.

"Is it me, or is this the most perfect day?"

She looked up at him, and snaked her arm around his back and drew him closer. He responded by putting an arm around her shoulder. Now they were strolling side-by-side, as close as could be, while the breakers threatened to soak their shoes.

"You're right," she said. "It really is the most perfect day."

They walked a little farther before Russ spoke again.

"I was thinking… when we put heart and soul into something, every experience is unforgettable."

Grace Chapman smiled. Once again, Russ Adams was right.

THE END

Thank you for reading
Life Begins at Sixty-Two and a Half.

I don't have a giant publishing house working on my behalf so I'm reliant on good people like yourself to help me spread the word about my books. If you enjoyed reading this one and have a few minutes to spare, I would be eternally grateful if you could leave a review on Amazon. For feel-good fiction authors like me, it's the only way we can gain traction for our books (which allows us to write more books). It would make me very happy indeed if you were able to say something nice.

Thank you!
Mark.

For more information about my books,
please visit my website:

www.markdaydy.co.uk

Printed in Great Britain
by Amazon